REAL MOVIE HERO

THE GREEN BROTHERHOOD: SEAL TEAM XII

DEBRA PARMLEY

*For all the men and women who step up,
when things go terribly wrong.*

*From the highly trained Navy SEAL, who protects and defends,
to the average citizen who carries and applies a tourniquet, to
save a life.*

This is what it is to love your neighbor.

This is what it takes to be a hero.

1

LITTLE CREEK, VIRGINIA

Reed "Railroad" Tindal aka "R.T." sat outside on the deck of Chicks bar, at the marina, enjoying his beer, as he and two of his SEAL brothers watched a boat pulling into one of the slips.

It was a perfect evening for sailing. Just enough of a breeze and the sun starting to set.

"That's the life," "Cutter" Antonius (Tony) said. "What I'm going to do after I retire. Nothing but sails, suds, and sweethearts."

"A girl for you in every port," Tanner "Diesel" Taylor said. "Not much different from what you have now."

Diesel liked to have a beer in every port, but Cutter, he was all about the women.

Around SEALs there were always women. Drawn to them like moths to flames.

A seagull landed on one of the posts near them and looked at them for food.

Sheri, their favorite cheerful dimpled waitress, showed up again to see if the men wanted another beer. "Fred has joined your party," she said. "Do you want some pretzels for him? And another beer?"

Reed shook his head. "Sorry, guys, I'd hang for another beer and to stay and chat," Reed said, "but I'm headed out to see a movie premiere."

"Oh, lucky you," Sheri said.

"Which one?" Diesel asked.

"*Turn and Deliver*, with Cole Kennick," Reed said.

"He's very handsome," Sheri said. "I like his movies."

"There should be plenty of good action scenes in that one," Cutter said. He raised his nearly empty glass. "And I'll take another beer, hun."

She smiled her dimpled grin at him. "You've got it."

"Cole Kennick does a better job keeping it real than most," Reed said.

"How'd you get passes?" Diesel asked.

"Won them from the local radio station," Reed said. "I've got one unclaimed pass." He turned to their waitress. "If you'd like to go, Sheri."

"You know I can't," Sheri shook her head. "My boyfriend wouldn't like that."

"It's just a movie," Reed said. "Not a kiss."

She put one hand on her hip. "Now you know that movies lead to kisses, and that is how people get into trouble."

"Are you saying you couldn't keep yourself from kissing me?" Reed teased.

Throwing one hand in the air she said, "Now you know that's not what I meant." Shaking her head, she turned and walked away.

"Well, guys, looks like I have one pass up for grabs if one of you wants it," Reed said.

"Can't tonight," Cutter said. "I'm meeting a chick here."

"That does not surprise me," Reed said.

"Another hot dancer with long legs?" Diesel asked.

Cutter grinned. "You know it."

The man was predictable as hell when it came to women, and he always seemed to be dating a dancer.

Reed turned to Diesel. "Do you want it?"

"Dad is flying in tonight, and I'm picking him up at the airport," Tanner "Diesel" Taylor said. "So, this is my limit tonight." He raised his beer. "And I've got to go." He drained his beer, and then pushed his chair back to stand.

Reed stood and said good night to both before heading toward the door.

Too bad the extra ticket would go to waste.

He'd just picked the tickets up from the station before heading to Chicks so there hadn't been time to ask around. Plus, he hadn't figured on both his brothers being busy tonight.

It was a weeknight, not a Saturday, and generally they all hung out at Chicks enjoying the views and brews. Tonight, it had just been the three of them.

It looked like he was headed to the premiere alone. But that didn't bother him. He would enjoy the movie either way.

~

"I can't go tonight," Tanya told Christie over the phone, her voice hard to hear, while Tanya's dog, Brutus, whined in the background, and her cat, Miss Priss, meowed mournfully. "There's no way I'll make the movie premiere. I hate to let you down, but it's crazy here."

"Oh, no," Christie said, her stomach dropping to her toes. "What's going on?"

Tanya is bailing.

Dismayed, Christie glanced at her watch. *We're supposed to meet in front of the theater in twenty minutes.*

The movie premiere passes Christie had won last week

from the local radio station were only good for tonight's premiere.

It's too late to call someone else.

Christie looked down at her red and white dress which showed off her curves.

And I'm dressed forties style. There's no time to change clothes.

The whole idea was she and Tanya were going to have a "girls' night out," dressed in 1940's attire. First, they'd see the movie, and then they'd go for drinks afterward. Both women enjoyed dressing in vintage fashions, and they'd each bought new dresses to show off.

Christie couldn't help but be disappointed.

Tanya interrupted Christie's thoughts. "Cole Kennick must be the hottest man in Hollywood, and you know how much I wanted to go to the premiere with you. But Miss Priss just yakked all over my bedspread, right after I finished cleaning up after Brutus. They're both sick. I'm thinking I might need to call the vet."

"I'm so sorry. Are they going to be all right?" Christie's concern for the animals pushed aside her disappointment at her best friend bailing on her. "Do you want me to come over?"

"No, I can handle this," Tanya said. "You go on to the movie. I don't want to be the reason you miss the premiere."

"What do you think it is?" Christie asked. "Did they both get into something? Maybe eat something bad?"

"They've eaten something I didn't give them, that much I do know," Tanya said. "What it is though, I can't tell."

"Oh my god." Christie didn't say her next thought.

Poison. The nasty neighbor might've poisoned them.

Tanya's neighbor was always complaining about Brutus and his barking. Brutus was a German Shepard and very protective of Tanya. Tanya's crazy neighbor jumped at any excuse to call the police. On the other hand, Miss Priss was a beautiful white Persian cat who never bothered anyone, although she did shed white hair everywhere.

"You'd better take a sample of the puke to the vet, in case he needs to test what they got into," Christie said.

"Already thought of that. Go enjoy the movie," Tanya said, her tone reassuring. "Don't worry. I don't want to ruin your fun evening."

"You're not going to ruin my evening," Christie said. "But I will miss you."

"Well, you'd better hurry or you'll be late," Tanya said. "And I don't think they let you in late to premieres."

Christie sighed. "All right, but I'm calling you just as soon as the movie is over."

"Thanks, Christie. And again, I'm so sorry about this."

"It's okay," Christie said. "You just take care of those sweet fur babies."

"Thanks for understanding," Tanya said.

"Hey, that's what best friends do," Christie said.

"Thanks bestie," Tanya said. "Chat soon. Don't be late!"

"I won't, "Christie said. "Bye."

"Bye."

Worrying about Tanya's fur babies, Christie grabbed the movie passes and hurried out the door to her car.

Fortunately, she made every streetlight by driving two miles under the speed limit and arrived just in time.

The line inside the Cinema One complex was long and filled the lobby. Christie stood at the end of line waiting.

At least I only need one seat.

Two ticket takers stood at the entrance. A man and a woman. The woman held a basket to collect their cell phones. She was explaining that everyone would get their phones back when they came out of the movie and she'd always be with the phones. Taking the phones was to prevent anyone from sneaking to take a video of the movie. The woman reminded everyone that pirating was against federal law.

Christie handed the man her pass and placed her phone into the basket the woman held. As she moved away, her gaze lingered on her phone reluctantly.

I hope Tanya won't need to reach me soon and that the vet tells Tanya her fur babies will be okay. She's got to do something about that mean neighbor. That woman has gone too far if she has poisoned them, and I'll bet she has. Poor Miss Priss and Brutus.

Inside, the theater was semi-dark and nearly full.

Christie stood at the bottom of the theater's stadium seating, letting her eyes adjust to the darkness and looking for one good seat.

Oh, there's one next to that fit, handsome man with the brown hair wearing the brown leather jacket.

Her gaze stopped and held as he captured her attention. His build was solid. Strong. Something about him drew her attention—and then she noticed, he was looking right back at her with his intense hazel eyes. But then, his gaze swept past her to the other side of the theater, as he sat quietly scanning the room.

Is he waiting for someone? Saving that seat? I hope not. It's a good location, and I'm running out of options.

She headed for the seat, hoping it would be free.

Reaching his isle, she leaned forward, drawing his full attention, and asked, "Is this seat taken?"

"No." He shook his head, his eyes watching her.

She smiled, and the teenager seated on the end of the aisle moved his feet, so she could slip between the rows.

"Excuse me," she said, and began the "theater row shuffle", being careful, as she was wearing her highest heels.

The new red ones, with the little bows on the front, and tall, narrow heels.

She'd had so much fun planning to glam it up on their girls' night out, and both she and Tanya had pretty dresses any pin-up girl would be proud of. Now, Tanya wouldn't see her in her new red and white checkered dress. The cool summer dress was form-fitting, and showed her curves, making her feel attractive, and glamorous, in a Marilyn Monroe kind of way.

All dolled up for a night on the town, and no one to spend it with.

There was no one here, that she knew, to see the dress and to appreciate it along with the time and effort she'd spent on her blonde hairdo, and makeup to complete the look. Plenty of men had ogled her since she'd stepped out of her car, in the theater parking lot, but that wasn't the kind of attention she wanted.

Tanya would've appreciated the dress, and the time it took to find the perfect dress, and to do her hair and makeup just so. Still, the entire row of men she passed, and men in the rows behind them, watched her every move.

Stepping daintily to the left of the handsome man in the brown leather jacket, and in front of the empty seat, she turned and sat while trying to play it cool, like she just needed a seat and not like she'd hoped to sit with him. Wondering where to put her purse and keeping in mind how a movie theater floor could be sticky, she bent and placed her new, shiny red purse on top of her feet, balancing it on her toes.

The air-conditioning sent a cool draft across her bare shoulders, bringing goose bumps, and making her want to shiver. She'd forgotten how cool the air could be in a theater when she'd ordered this dress. Wishing she'd worn a shawl; Christie hoped all the people in the theater would create enough body heat to warm the room up. At least when she leaned back against the seat, the vent blew in front of her, not on her back. Though her neck and collarbone were receiving the draft, chilling her front side.

Now that she was seated, she realized how much taller than her the handsome man was. Sitting next to him made her feel downright delicate. His chest, shoulders, and arms were muscular, and he exuded strength.

Oh my, but he's handsome, and he smells good.

She glanced down at his hand.

No wedding ring. I wonder why he's here without a date, or a friend? Women probably fall all over him. I wonder what his name is.

On her other side, a large man in an orange T-shirt and jeans sat holding a huge tub of popcorn. "Here by yourself?" he said. "That's terrible."

Taken aback by his sly tone, she leaned away from the nosy man and closer to the handsome man, aware of him now watching her and the nosy man.

"Why would you ask?" she said, frowning and then catching herself, as she decided she shouldn't be speaking to this stranger about whether she was out alone. "That's none of your business," she said, feeling herself bristle.

Maybe this seat wasn't such a good one after all.

Though the view of the screen was excellent, and she was near enough to the aisle to get out without having to climb over half a row of people, now she hoped the nosy man wouldn't continue to bother her.

Mr. Nosy leaned forward, as if to say something else, and his hand reached toward her, but then he stopped, looking past her to handsome man.

She turned to glance at handsome man, wondering what he'd done to stop Mr. Nosy.

Handsome Man's hair was damp, likely from having

taken a recent shower. Hot as it was outside, his hair would've dried otherwise. She became aware once again of his aftershave or cologne, a manly enticing scent.

"Most people are here because they received a pass to the premiere," the handsome man said dryly.

Mr. Nosy shut up and went back to eating his popcorn, taking a huge handful.

Christie exhaled stress she didn't know she'd been holding.

Better Mr. Nosy keeps his attention on his popcorn, and not on me.

"Thank you," Christie whispered under her breath, just low enough the handsome man could hear.

"No problem," came his low answer.

He smells good.

And that low voice was doing things to her insides as his scent assaulted her senses on another level. Pheromones flooded her body, making her aware of her breath, her heartbeat, the way her palms were starting to warm. The slight flush in her pale cheeks and chest, which always happened, would begin now.

Her pheromones could get her into trouble sometimes when they kicked in before she figured out if a guy was a good man to be with or not.

As the lights began to dim, she thought, *Good thing we'll be in a dark theater. Handsome Man will never know how I'm reacting to him.*

～

R eed Tindal sat scanning the crowd.

Attentiveness was by now an ingrained habit, though he was casual about it, unless he needed not to be.

A trained SEAL, when he was awake, he was always aware of his surroundings.

The pretty blonde with the creamy skin and stunning green eyes had caught his attention before she'd noticed him. Then, their gazes had connected, and he'd felt that flicker, the one that always happened when attraction kicked in. This attraction was strong. Strong enough to take him by surprise, as she usually wouldn't have been his type.

She was wearing a delicate red and white checked dress with little straps and high heels.

With soft blonde shoulder length curls tied with a red ribbon, smokey eyeliner, and cherry red lipstick, she was girly from her head to her red painted toenails, which peeked out of her shoes. Those red high heeled shoes with red bows on the front were the kind that always made him wonder how a woman would run if she had to, without turning an ankle. He hoped this beauty never found out. She turned heads dressed like that, and some heads were best avoided.

He wondered what her story was, and why she was all dressed up to watch a movie by herself. There was a story there. He couldn't imagine any hot-blooded male standing up a woman who looked as good as she did.

Reed was used to dating women who were more practical. Sensible about things like shoes, wore jeans instead of dresses, and carried guns. There was nowhere on that pretty dress where this woman could carry a gun or anything else. In fact, he'd bet she didn't even know how to shoot a gun.

She looked like the "take care of me" type, not the "I'll take care of things myself" type.

Everyone was seated. A man in a black suit stepped onto the stage and welcomed them to the premiere, then the lights were dimmed, and everyone settled in to watch the show.

The blonde, caught up in the story, would catch her breath, only to release it when Cole escaped the bad guy's malevolence, and avoided getting so much as a mark on him.

Her breathy sighs and little gasps caught Reed's attention each time, though he was also focusing on the movie. He was good at doing two things at once.

The movie held her complete attention, and she seemed unaware of anything else, though Reed had noted her initial reaction to him.

Reed could have been caught up in the movie as well if he'd let himself. Cole was one of the few actors who did their own stunts, and he kept his movies more real than most. Which meant Reed didn't disengage and start critiquing action shots five minutes into the movie.

Had he been at home, he might have been as caught up as the woman was. But out in public, nothing would ever take up his total attention. However, that was not to say he wasn't enjoying the movie. In fact, he was enjoying the movie as well as her reactions to it.

Total opposites, he thought as he noted her reactions to the movie. She was so caught up in the movie, she didn't notice anything else.

Reed had grown up in a neighborhood where boys had to fight, or be picked on, so he'd learned early on to fight, and to pay attention to who was where, always. He viewed her as he would a child, or any other innocent civilian, who hadn't learned to be wary. He was glad to see her relaxing and enjoying the movie.

This was why men like him fought. To protect the innocent, and preserve a peaceful way of life, and freedom. These were some of the reasons he fought.

Actor Cole Kennick played roles in which he did the

same, which was one reason Reed enjoyed watching his movies.

Some feeling he couldn't have named, other than to call it a sixth sense, made him turn his focus to a man at the front of the theater, dressed all in black.

Not one of the staff.

Another patron, perhaps.

He stood at the far-right corner of the theater. Something about him was very off.

The man turned to face the crowd, and began to move his arm upward —

Damn.

Reed went calm and cool, even as he thought the word, his training kicking in, knowing the man was going to shoot.

Everything around Reed slowed.

"Everyone down!" he yelled, as his hand landed on the pretty blonde's shoulder, forcing her to the ground behind the seats.

The shooter raised his gun to fire.

2

Christie didn't understand what was happening, as the handsome man next to her shouted, and the sharp reports of gunfire — not coming from the screen, but somewhere in the theater - erupted. At the same time, the man's strong, warm hand closed over her bare shoulder, hard, pulling her away from her seat, pushing her forward and down onto her knees on the sticky theater floor.

"Stay down," he said, his tone brisk and harsh.

His right hand reached for the gun he carried in a belt holster behind his back. "Stay here."

She followed his directions, crouching low, with her hands over her head, so scared she was shaking, but she couldn't resist looking at the shooter through the small space between the seats.

Dressed in a black hoodie, she saw only his tall, lean figure and a long gun pointing toward them.

Oh my God. We're all going to die. Her thoughts raced as the shots continued. *I'm not ready, Lord. Please don't let me die now.*

The handsome man leapt over the seats in front of them,

firing, up and over the crowd, his aim deadly, his body moving in a straight line, charging the shooter.

The man in black went down.

The confrontation was over in seconds, which dragged like minutes. Less time than any of them would have guessed, other than Reed, who'd been well trained to eliminate this kind of threat. He knew what could happen in just a few seconds, and exactly how fast he needed to be.

Reed hoped like hell that nobody had been killed. The shooter had gotten off a few shots before he went down.

Women's screams still filled the air along with crying.

A man called out, "I've been shot."

The screaming stopped.

There was a moment of silence, following the gunshots, which gave Reed a chance to take a deep breath and added to his sense of calm.

A few people raised their heads to look at the shooter.

Sounds of women crying replaced the silence.

A man moaned.

Reed reached into his left pocket, as his right thumb pressed a button on his gun.

The empty magazine fell to the ground, as he slapped in a new one, and kept moving forward, down to where the gunman lay on the floor.

He'd make sure the man didn't get up and start shooting again. He had to make sure he'd delivered the kill shot he thought he had. He'd take no chances.

First thing he did, was kick away, and remove all weapons, out of the man's reach. Then he bent to check the man's pulse.

Nothing. The man was dead.

Reed pulled out his cell phone, and dialed 911, thankful he'd ignored instructions to hand his phone in along with all the others.

Likely, he was the only one in the theater able to call. Something the shooter had probably counted on. Like counting on all the patrons to be unarmed.

"Springfield dispatch," a female voice answered.

"I need to report the live shooter at Springfield Cinema One, is now down," he said.

"A live shooter at Springfield Cinema One," the voice repeated. "Did you say down?"

"Yes," he said. "One live shooter down. No others in sight."

"Who am I speaking to?"

"Reed Tindal. I'm a Navy SEAL."

"Are you armed, Mr. Tindal?"

"Yes. One patron has been shot. I'll assess and report back. We're going to need at least two ambulances."

"Please stay on the line, Mr. Tindal. Police and ambulances are on their way."

"Roger that."

He moved back to where the pretty blonde was still crouching on the ground.

She looked up at him, her eyes wide.

"You can get up now," he said. "It's safe."

She rose, slowly and shakily. "Safe," she repeated, as if to reassure herself.

"Yes," he answered. "You're safe. What's your name?"

"Christie Anderson."

"Okay Christie." He handed her his phone. "Take this. Stay on the line with dispatch. I'm going to check on the wounded."

The blonde blinked, as if waking from a fog, but then took the phone. "Of course."

"Good," he said.

She put his phone to her ear and then said, "Hello?"

"Where is Mr. Tindal?" the dispatcher asked, "And who

am I speaking to?"

Mr. Tindal, that was his name.

She filed his name away in her memory as the man who'd saved her life. "He's checking for wounded, but I'll stay on the line," Christie said. "I'm Christie Anderson."

"All right, Christie. Stay with me until the police arrive. And let me know what is happening."

"Yes, ma'am."

Christie watched Mr. Tindal moving quickly, his glance going up and down aisles, while he reassured theater patrons that everything was over, and would be okay now. His expression hardened when he found the man who'd called out he'd been shot.

The dispatcher asked, "Ask Mr. Tindal how many are injured?"

"Okay," Christie said. "Hang on. I have to move down to where he is, right now. He's with a man who got shot."

"Keep talking to me," the dispatcher said. "Tell me what's happening."

"Well, I won't really know, 'til I get down there," Christie said.

"Okay, just stay on the line."

"I will." Christie started moving down toward where Mr. Tidal was.

The wounded man who'd shouted out, was in a theater seat, and Mr. Tindal was getting the nearby patrons to move out of the way, so he could get to him.

As Christie got nearer, she saw the man had been shot in the arm. Blood was everywhere, and the man's skin was pale, as if he'd already lost too much blood. The man in the row behind him, was also shot, bleeding from his arm.

She breathed in sharp, the images nearly stopping her.

The dispatcher, who'd been listening said, "What is it? Christie, are you all right?"

Nausea hit her stomach, and she pressed her free hand to her belly, to try to calm it back down. She couldn't get sick at the sight of blood, she had to pull herself together.

"Yes." She swallowed hard. "There's just a lot of blood. Two men have been shot. I'm down here with Mr. Tindal now."

Mr. Tindal pulled something out of his pocket, and then started to unwind a strap of some kind. He opened the thing into what looked like a circle.

"He's got something he's making into a circle," Christie said.

"That's probably a tourniquet."

"I feel like I should be helping him," Christie said.

"Do you have any medical training?"

"No," she said.

"If he's a SEAL, he may have been trained as a medic. He'll know what to do, until the ambulance arrives. You just stay on the line."

Christie could hear sirens in the distance. "I hear sirens now."

"They're almost there. You just hang on."

Christie reached Mr. Tindal.

He glanced up and gave her a nod. "Put the call on speaker, then put it down and help me."

"Okay." She tapped the speaker setting and said, "You're on speaker phone now, so you can hear us both. I need to help him."

"Tell me what's happening," the dispatcher said.

Mr. Tindal responded, "We've got two men shot, both in the arm. Need tourniquets. I've got two with me."

He reached into his pocket, pulled out a second tourniquet, and handed it to Christie. "You're going to put this one on that guy, while I put one on this guy."

Christie stared at him with wide eyes.

"I don't know anything about tourniquets."

"It's not hard," Mr. Tindal said. "Open it up. And hurry."

Looking at it, Christie found the ends, and let the rest of the band fall, opening easily into a circle.

She hurried into the isle behind the first wounded man, and saw blood all over the second man, and on the empty seat that had been cleared, so Mr. Tindal could get to him.

But Mr. Tindal was only one man and he'd said to hurry.

"Now, put it on his arm," Mr. Tindal said. "Get as high up as you can get, without going up onto his shoulder."

The wounded man whimpered, as Christie awkwardly complied, squatting on her high heels, trying not to cause more pain.

"Now what?" he said.

"You need to cinch it down tight," Mr. Tindal said. "Watch me."

Christie paid close attention as Mr. Tindal tightened the strap, doubled it back, and then began twisting a metal rod, like a windlass, before looping it into a strap of Velcro.

Mr. Tindal looked her in the eyes. "It needs to be as tight as possible. Better to hurt him now than to let him bleed to death."

Christie felt the blood drain from her face.

The only way to get enough leverage to turn that tourniquet properly, the way Mr. Tindal was doing, was to kneel on the bloody seat, next to the man who'd been shot, and put her weight into it.

Her new dress would be ruined. But she had to do it anyway.

She turned back to the man she was working on, her hands fumbling on their own.

This near to the man, the stench of blood made her stomach roil, but she pressed on.

Christie tightened the strap, then started twisting the

windlass.

With each turn, the man's face screwed up tighter in pain, but she didn't stop until it was too tight for her to turn. Then she strapped it down.

Mr. Tindal watched her, appraisingly, and then nodded his approval.

Good. She exhaled. *I must have done it right. I hope this man makes it.*

"Both tourniquets are on," Mr. Tindal said into the phone. "ETA on those ambulances?"

"Three minutes," the dispatcher said.

When he set the phone down, Christie said, "It's a good thing you had two of those."

"I always carry two tourniquets," he said. "Because we have two femoral arteries."

"Oh," Christie said.

She knew little about anatomy, and wasn't sure where femoral arteries were, but was glad he knew, and that he knew what to do.

"By the way, you did a great job," he said.

Blushing, she glanced down. "Thank you," she said, embarrassed by his praise.

Police officers streamed into the theater, alert, armed and ready for trouble.

Mr. Tindal sat back on his heels, having finished with the civilian he'd been treating.

The first officer approached him and said, "Reed Tindal?"

"That's me." He nodded at the man he'd just treated. "This one is wounded, and there's another." He pointed to the other man.

The officer nodded. "Are you armed?"

"Yes," Mr. Tindal stood slowly. "Behind my right hip."

"Ok. I'm going to ask you step out of the isle, and down

the stairs."

Christie noted that the police officers had arrived with guns drawn. They'd eased off but not holstered their weapons.

Mr. Tindal obeyed, moving out of the isle, and down the stairs, followed by the first officer.

Was all this necessary? Couldn't they see he wasn't the bad guy? He was the man who'd stopped the bad guy. Everyone in the theater owed their lives to Mr. Tindal.

"Turn and face the wall, please," the officer said.

Mr. Tindal automatically pressed his palms against the wall and didn't seem upset.

"This the gun you used tonight?"

"Yes sir," Mr. Tindal said. "It's reloaded. Habit."

"Right," the officer said.

Mr. Tindal waited in silence, as the officer disarmed him, and looked at the gun.

Reed faced the wall, and then waited for the officer to follow procedure. Now that the police were here, he could stand down. He waited, as the officer disarmed him, and thoughts of Christie ran through his head.

As Reed had watched Christie appraisingly, he'd reassessed his first impression of her.

It was always a make-or-break moment, especially for civilians who'd never seen this kind of thing before.

Most people were much more capable than they thought, and it always cheered him to see them realize it.

This petite, throwback blonde had done better than many soldiers he'd seen reacting to carnage their first time. She listened well, didn't question what had to be done, and did it to the best of her ability.

Maybe she isn't as much of a "take care of me" type female as she appears to be. She hadn't fallen apart. She'd followed directions without getting emotional.

Though not the "Step up, I'll take care of things myself" type of female, perhaps there's more to her than just her looks and femininity. She's willing and capable of taking care of others.

Now she intrigued him. He wanted to get to know her better, find out more about her.

However, this wasn't the time.

He waited for the officer to finish.

His Sig Sauer P229 had been properly de-cocked, and the hammer was down. The officer had only to unload it.

"I've also got a knife on my ankle," he said, knowing a pat down was the procedure, and it was best to tell where any weapons were, so he could be disarmed.

"Thank you," the officer said, after patting him down, and removing the knife. "You can turn around now."

"Thanks," Reed said. He'd expected all this and wasn't concerned by it. Now they'd have to wait for detectives, and crime scene investigators to arrive, and then he'd have to answer a lot of questions.

He didn't look forward to that part, and what would turn into a long night.

Reed glanced over to where Christie was, to see how she was doing.

She was sitting quietly, while a female officer spoke to her. The bottom of her dress, and her hose,where her knees had met the bloody seat cushion, were stained with blood.

Too bad her dress had been ruined. She looked hot in that dress.

The EMP's were here now, bringing in stretchers for the wounded men.

Everyone made way for them.

There wasn't much room in a theater for two stretchers, and the wounded men were in theater seats, but they made it work, and soon the two men were out of the theater, and on their way to the emergency room.

Now the detectives would really get to work, and the questioning would begin.

Christie didn't remember much more than a blur of color and sound, after it was all over.

There were uniformed police, white-shirted EMT's, and paramedics, and detectives in business casual suits—all of them asking questions.

Are you all right? Where were you sitting? What happened next? What did you hear? Did he say anything? How many shots...

She mumbled out what she could remember.

There was a big gap, where she'd been too petrified with fear, to move, or to think.

Then after, she remembered Mr. Tindal asking for her help, handing her his phone, and the tourniquets. Following what he told her, and copying what he was doing, to save a life.

She'd done that. She too had saved a life.

It all seemed surreal now. Hard to believe it had happened, though it had.

When there was nothing left to tell, and she'd been wrung completely dry, a detective finally gave her a business card, and said, "Go home and get some rest. We'll be in touch."

Christie numbly took the card, said, "Yes, sir," and turned to leave.

Someone holding the basket with all the patrons remaining cell phones held the basket out to her, and invited her to find her phone.

It was the only phone still in the basket with a pink cover.

She picked the phone up. "That's mine," she said, before dropping the phone in her purse, without looking at it.

She moved toward the door as if through a foggy night.

As she passed Mr. Tindal, who was still being questioned, she heard the detective thank him for helping.

"It could a been a lot worse. You saved a lot of people here tonight," he said.

"Just doing my job." Mr. Tindal shrugged, as if this was the kind of thing he did every day.

But then, for a Navy SEAL, maybe it was.

～

Christie got behind the wheel of her car, and sat still for several minutes before moving.

Inside the pale blue Chevy, it was quiet.

No one was talking; no one was moving about. There were no people who'd been shot, and needed tourniquets. There were no women screaming, and no gunshots being fired. There were no more men shot, and nearly dying. There was no bad guy on the floor, who might get up again to hurt more people.

The quiet in the car calmed everything, in a way the quiet in the theater never had, but she only briefly registered what it was doing.

She simply sat, while the police lights flashed silently.

And then, after a while, she started the car, without really thinking, and began the drive toward home.

The red light on her dash, which reminded her to get gas, was still on.

Gas. That's right. I need gas. Now. Won't make it home.

She drove until she saw the first gas station on her route, one she'd never been to before, and pulled in.

Pulling up to the pump, she parked and turned off her car.

Her purse had fallen off the seat, onto the floor.

She unbuckled her seatbelt, and then leaned down to

get it. Taking her purse, she reached in for her wallet, found her credit card, and then got out of the car.

She moved to the back of the car, and opened the fuel door, then unscrewed the fuel cap, and let it hang by its cord. She turned toward the pump, and stopped in front of it, to insert her credit card, but with her hand shaking, she missed, and dropped the card on the ground.

As Reed drove down the street, he saw Christie's red and white dress, as she stood on those high red heels at the gas pump, getting ready to put gas into her car. A pale blue Chevy.

She bent down to pick up something on the ground.

What is she thinking? This is a bad area of town for a woman alone to pump gas, especially wearing an outfit like that. Every man in the gas station parking lot is watching her bend over in that dress. Damn. Didn't she see the graffiti on the fence, beside the gas station?

This is the wrong station for her to be stopping at to get gas, at any time of day, but especially at this time of night.

He pulled into the gas station behind her, and turned off his car to get out.

She'd attracted the attention of a group of men, who hovered at the edge of the building, near a parked black mustang with dark windows, and a beat-up old white van.

One man with tattoos on his neck and face gave a whistle as she bent down.

Another, a tall, thin, bald man with tattoos on his neck, who wore a tattered jean jacket, moved toward her.

She was focused on the credit card, trying to insert it into the machine, and failing.

She didn't seem to notice the men watching her, while nudging each other, laughing as their man moved toward her.

3

———

Reed got out, and closed his door. He stepped purposefully toward her.

"Hey, Christie," he said, as he moved closer. "Let me give you a hand with that."

He noted the bald man stopped, realizing Reed was with her, and then turned to walk back to his group.

Christie stood, looking way too fragile, and feminine, as her hand holding the card shook.

Her wide green eyes looked up at him in surprise, when he called out to her, but she seemed not to recognize him, at first.

Then her eyes widened. "Oh. Yes. Hello, Mr. Tindal"

"Reed," he said. "Reed Tindal." His hand closed over hers, and he held it for a moment, to still the shaking. He noted that her hand was cold inside his, and he gave her a warm smile.

Then, glancing down at the card, he said, "It's backward."

"Oh. Yes, it is. Thank you," she said.

"You're welcome," he said.

She pulled her hand away, turned the card around, and

then tried to insert it again, but her hand still had the shakes.

"Let me do that," he said.

She handed him the card.

He put it into the machine, and then it asked for her code. "Your turn," he said.

She paused, as if thinking, as a frown came over her face.

Maybe she didn't trust him.

He turned his head, toward the men, giving her a chance to put the code in privately, without him seeing the numbers.

Lowering his voice, so the men could not hear him, he asked, "Did those guys scare you?"

"Guys? What guys?"

He turned back to look more closely at her.

Christie is in bad shape if she hasn't noticed the guys clearly watching her every move.

Had she even heard that whistle? Seen the man approaching her from less than ten feet away?

As Reed watched her, he noted she had no awareness of her surroundings; her only focus was on getting gas.

He had to remind himself, she was a civilian with likely no understanding of situational awareness.

And the men were still watching her, and now, him.

"No problem," he said. "Why don't you go on and get in your car, while I finish this."

"Okay," she said.

The men's interest in her hadn't waned, though they were watching, and talking among themselves.

They hadn't made another step toward her.

He doubted they would, now.

Reed had found that after SEAL training, few men

messed with him. Only the rare asshole, looking for a fight, would pursue one.

Usually, Reed could de-escalate things with his calm response.

He didn't want to fight unless he had to, but when he did fight, he fought to end things fast. His goal was to put the other man down fast, so peace could resume.

The calm confidence he always displayed could easily be read by any man with street smarts.

You never took your eyes off the calm man in the back, because that calm man was likely the one who would take you down fast, and hard.

The group of men, though they watched, made no other move toward her, or him. Likely, they'd also noted the stickers on his car, one which let him drive his car on base, and the other a SEAL bone frog sticker.

Reed watched her get into her car.

She was safe once again.

He put the nozzle into the gas tank, and started filling it.

Christie rolled down her window.

He wondered why her hand had been shaking, if she wasn't afraid of the men.

Is she still shaken up, after the shooting? She shouldn't be out here alone like this, on any night, let alone this one.

Now that her window was down, they could talk again.

"So, how are you doing?" He watched her, looking for signs of shock.

The EMTs had been busy tonight, with a theater full of people to check out, and maybe they'd missed seeing her.

He'd been busy, and hadn't paid attention to what was going on with Christie.

She hadn't been shot, and had seemed fine. She'd been right there by his side, helping him with triage, intently listening, and following his orders, so he'd assumed she was fine.

And maybe she had been then, but she clearly wasn't fine now.

"I-I'm okay. Just...cold." She shrugged, and rubbed her hands up and down her arms.

The thing was, it wasn't cold out tonight.

Humidity made his leather jacket too warm, and there wasn't even a breeze.

He would've frowned, but held that back, and kept a casual, pleasant expression on his face. "You were headed home?"

He hoped that was the case.

"Yes. I-I was running late to the premiere, and had meant to stop for gas," Christie said. "But I was going to be too late, if I got gas then, so I didn't stop. When I came out, I remembered that I didn't have enough to get home, without stopping."

"If you'd said something, I'd have followed you, to make sure you were safe," he said. "I'll finish here, and then follow you home. Make sure you get inside safe."

"Oh, thank you. That's nice of you." She placed her hand on his arm, and turned her green eyes up to him. "Thank you again, for saving my life."

Her slim delicate fingers were cool upon his arm.

Shock was his assessment.

"Any time," he said, and then, redirecting her, added, "You okay to drive home? You still look a little shaken up."

"I'm okay now," she said. "I can drive."

He wasn't so sure. "How far is it?"

"About twenty minutes."

He'd have preferred knowing miles, as that's what he'd asked her, but wasn't going to press her on it.

If she were like his cousin, Katelyn, she wouldn't have any idea how many miles.

Christie didn't seem like a practical sort of woman.

Girly from head to toe, she was the kind who needed looking after. An innocent. The kind bad men would pounce on, if someone weren't protecting her.

The someone tonight being him, which he didn't mind in the least. It was in his nature to protect.

Though she wasn't the sort he usually went out with, and this wasn't a date now, he felt a strong need to protect her, as if she were his, under his protection.

It seemed she brought that out in him.

Perhaps the live shooting event they'd been through together had created a bond, as intense situations tended to do; a friendship, if nothing more, though he liked her.

He liked her enough to want to ask her out, and get to know her better.

She was rubbing her arms, and the movement moved the low-cut neckline of her dress.

He admired the view, but he wasn't the only one in this parking lot watching her, and he wanted her out of here, and home safe again.

She smiled at him. "This is nice of you. To stop, and help me get gas, and to follow me home."

Finishing, he closed and twisted the lid on the gas tank, pushed the cover over top of it, and then walked back around to her open window.

She sat inside, with her hands resting on the bottom of the steering wheel.

From his vantage point, he could see down into her cleavage. His gaze went there, though he hadn't intended it to.

The view teased. Her soft curves looked touchable, and

enticing. He'd have loved to see more of her breasts. Just as any other red-blooded male would have.

Looking up at him, with those green eyes, she said, "Thank you. I appreciate you helping me with the gas."

"You're welcome," he said. "Are you ready to drive?"

"Yes," she nodded. "I'm ready."

"Then start her up. I'm right behind you."

"Okay," she said.

He walked back to his car, and she started hers.

Soon, they were driving the roads which led to her house.

She drove slowly, five miles under the speed limit, like someone who hadn't had enough sleep, or was driving home from a party, after a few too many.

His concern for her made his brow furrow, as he wondered at her state of mind.

It was a good thing he'd seen her on his way home and had stopped.

Her house was on a street where older cottage-style houses lined both sides, and well-groomed trees stood in the grassy areas of the median.

She pulled onto her driveway and parked.

Her house was painted white, had soft blue shutters, and a black roof.

Blue and purple flowers out front had taken over in an explosion of color.

He pulled in behind her, as she opened her car door. He got out of his car, and walked up beside her. "Nice house," he said.

"I've lived here for three years," she said. "I love it."

"I can tell," he said and smiled. "I take it you enjoy gardening, and flowers."

"Flowers? Oh, I'm all about flowers." She giggled.

Is she nervous, or is there something funny that I missed?

"Oh, I didn't tell you." She stopped, putting her hand to her mouth. "I'm a florist. Flowers surround me all day. At work, here at home . . ."

He laughed. "So, you do enjoy flowers."

"That's a big understatement." She laughed. "I love flowers. And I love arranging them."

"That's great." He grinned.

Her excitement was good to see, and her happiness contagious.

He'd also managed to take her mind off of tonight's live shooting event, and onto a happier topic. "I'll have to stop into your shop some time."

"Oh yes, you should." She nodded. "I work at Floral Blessings, the new shop by the library. I used to work for a wedding planner, doing the big jobs, but now I'm in with Mrs. Brown, who really ought to be named Mrs. White, because she's so pale. She's a short, white haired, sixty-eight-year-old widow. After her husband died, she decided to start a new career selling flowers. She smiles all the time. You'd never know she was widowed less than two years ago."

They'd reached Christie's front door, as they walked and talked, and she automatically reached into her purse for her keys.

After about a minute of rifling through her purse, she pulled them out. The keys hung from a red and white polka dotted key chain.

He held the screen door for her, while she fumbled with the key in the lock. All the while he watched her, he noted she showed symptoms of shock.

"Come in for coffee?" she asked. "It's the least I can do, after all you've done for me."

It was late and they both needed sleep, not coffee, but he suspected she wasn't ready to be alone, or ready to go to sleep.

He certainly wasn't.

Maybe she'd quit thanking him if he allowed her to thank him with coffee. It would also give them a chance to get to know each other better. "Sounds good," he said.

"I have some Jamaican blue," she said. "Got it on a cruise, and I save it for special occasions."

"Sounds wonderful," he said. "Where did you cruise to?"

"Jamaica, of course," she said with a grin. "Grand Cayman, and also Saint Thomas. Have you ever been?"

"Nope." He shook his head. "Been lots of places around the world, but nothing in the Caribbean yet. No pleasure cruising."

"The islands are wonderful," she said. "Very relaxing."

"That sounds good, right about now," he said.

"I agree." She smiled and nodded.

As she busied herself making coffee, he took in the room.

White lace curtains hung above the window over the sink, and the window in the back door, a white lace table-cloth covered a small, round table, and padded cushions with a pale pink and white polka dotted print sat atop the two chairs.

The pale pink was picked up in accessories throughout the white kitchen; accessories that could've stepped out of an old movie, where the woman of the house wore an apron and a dress.

She noticed him looking and said, "I love anything retro, from the forties and fifties."

Ah. So that's why she's dressed like that, and why her house is decorated this way.

"It suits you," he said.

Those boys overseas would've had many a good dream about her, if a poster of her in that dress, were pinned in their locker.

"Thank you." She rubbed her hands down her hips, in a

self-conscious gesture; unaware she outlined her hips, drawing his gaze to those curves.

"I, well, this is why I'm dressed like this," she said. "Tanya and I were having a girl's night out, retro style. I'd step back in time, if I could, and visit those days."

"You look great."

"Thank you." Pink flooded her cheeks.

Is she embarrassed? Not used to compliments.

"Who is Tanya?" he asked.

"She's my best friend," Christie said.

He frowned. "You were alone tonight. What happened to Tanya?"

"She had an emergency with her animals. Had to take them to the vet. I think her neighbor poisoned them." She gasped. "Oh, no. I was supposed to call her, after the show. I didn't think to check my phone. Oh, I hope they're all right."

She hurried to her purse, and pulled her phone out, turning it back on, and watching for it to turn on again.

Ding. Ding. Ding.

Her phone was blowing up with missed calls or texts, likely from people who cared about her, and had heard about the shooting at the theater.

Christie sat on a kitchen chair, her shoulders dropping. She read through text after text.

Reed tried not to appear nosy, or to look, but it was clear she was upset again. "Lots of messages. Everything okay?"

"Miss Priss and Brutus are going to be okay. They both ate something bad that I've never heard of. I hope it's not a poison. And Tanya is worried about me. She heard on the news about the shooting."

"Maybe you should call her," he said.

"After coffee. I promised you coffee. And she's probably asleep now." Christie put her phone down, and got back up

to get two coffee mugs out. She glanced back over her shoulder. "Sugar? Cream?"

"Black."

"Okay." She placed the coffee mugs on the table, and
then got dream and sugar out for herself. "It's almost ready."

Pouring the coffee, her hands trembled again, making
the coffee slosh over the side of the cup.

"Hey," he closed his hand over hers "You're still shaking.
Let me."

4

———

Christie nodded as the warmth of Reed's hand grounded her, and eased the shaking in her hand.

His warm hazel gaze met hers.

Letting him take the coffee pot from her, to pour, she then sat, some of the stress easing.

"That shooting shook me too," he said, as he poured the coffee into the other cup.

"I never would've guessed," she said. "You seemed so calm, and knew just what to do."

"I wasn't expecting it," he said, "But I've been trained in how to react."

"You knew what to do," she said. "I'm so glad you did."

"Me too," he said, giving her a smile, his warm gaze making her feel safe and secure.

Everything about him seemed warm, safe, and caring.

She needed that warmth.

She stirred the sugar and cream into her coffee, and then sat for a while, taking in his warmth without speaking, as they each sipped from their coffee cups.

His silent companionship was nice.

She really did not want to be alone, right now.

Just sitting near him reassured her.

Finally, he spoke. "Want to talk about it?"

She nodded, and then tried to find the words. "It was…" she paused, unable to articulate what she wanted to say. "I don't have the word for it."

"You're not used to gunfire," he said. "I am. Very used to it. But it shook me, too."

She shook her head. "You didn't seem shaken. You took charge. Your military training. You took care of everyone."

"Yes. With your help." He spoke quiet, watching her. "My training has given me a faster reaction time. But it still takes time for the brain to process what is happening, and to act, even for a trained soldier."

"You seemed pretty fast to me," she said. "You saved my life, pushed me down, before you even started shooting. I owe you my life."

"No." He shook his head. "You owe me nothing. There's no debt owed."

"Then you have my undying gratitude, and thanks," she said.

"Christie, this is what I do," he said. "What I'm trained to do. For a Navy SEAL, taking bad guys out is just part of the job."

"You're a Navy SEAL?" Her jaw dropped as her estimation of him rose way, way, up, beyond where it was already.

He was like a hero stepped out of a movie screen, a real movie hero, not an actor, and this did more than confirm it.

It set this fact in concrete.

He was a true hero, trained to be one of those guys who the military sent in to handle the toughest, most dangerous jobs.

"Yes," he said.

"Wow. I'm impressed," she said, her eyes wide. "I'm so

glad you were there. I'm glad you're trained to do what you do and that you do it so well. And I'm just happy to be alive."

"Hey, I'm with you on that one," he said. "Happy to be alive." He winked at her. "Now, how about we enjoy our coffee, and get to know each other a little better."

"Okay," she smiled. "That sounds good."

"Where are you from?" he asked.

"I'm from a little town in Pennsylvania that no one has ever heard of," she said.

"Try me."

"Gouldsboro, PA. ," she said. "In the Pocono Mountains. There's not even a flashing red light, and it's thirty minutes to the nearest grocery store."

He laughed. "No wonder no one's heard about it. How did you end up here?"

"I couldn't wait to get off that mountain, and wanted to see more of the world, so I picked a college farther away, and moved." She smiled.

"Didn't finish my degree, but I made it through three years, before I ran out of money. Then I started working for a wedding planner. Found out I loved working with flowers more than going to classes for a degree, so I finished the semester, and then never went back."

Wow, I'm just rambling, giving him way more information than he asked for.

He's so easy to talk to, and I'm nervous, and talking too much.

I need to ask him things, and not just talk about myself. "What about you? Where are you from?"

"Texas, my first nine years," he said. "And then Florida until my senior year of high school. I joined the U.S. Navy after graduation, with the goal of becoming a SEAL."

"Why are you here now, and not off on a mission?"

"I'm stateside for now," he said. "After my grandfather

passed. I had leave built up, so I'm here for a while to help my mom out."

"I'm so glad you were here tonight."

"I'm glad too," he said.

Their gazes met, searching and connecting, as the chemistry between them sizzled again, his male strength, and her inviting softness.

"I'm glad you're here with me now. You make me feel safe." Her voice came out soft, and she blushed.

His voice did things to her. And she was glad he was here. She wished he would stay. Wished he didn't have to go. But she would never ask him to stay. She'd just met him.

They finished their coffee, and when he stood, she followed, looking up at him.

"I'd better tell you good night," he said. "It's been nice getting to know you, Christie. Thanks for the coffee."

"It was the least I could do when you—"

He placed a finger on her lips, to silence her from thanking him again, as she was going to do.

She smiled beneath it.

His finger, warm and gentle on her lips, made her mind move from what she was about to say, to the new sensations he was creating.

He let his finger drop. "I'm glad we met, and I'm glad you're safe at home. You get some rest, and be sure to lock the door behind me."

"Yes," she said.

She was tempted to say, "Yes, sir," as his last words had a ring of command to them, in a concerned, "I'm just looking out for you" kind of way. Like her grandfather used to do.

Maybe it was because both men had served in the military and had learned the art of command.

Whatever it was, it made her feel very cared for. She didn't mind complying with that kind of command.

Reed walked with her to the door, noting the way she moved. When he reached it, he said, "When do you have to go back to work?"

"Monday," she said.

"You don't have to go anywhere today?" This being Sunday, he hoped that was the case.

She shook her head, "No."

"Good," he said. "Get some rest now."

"I will. Good night. Or good morning," she said.

She looked confused.

The sun was up, and it was morning.

"Or good day," she said.

"Good everything," he said with a grin. "See you later, Christie Anderson."

She grinned back. "See you later, Reed Tindal."

Reed turned and started for his car, but his ears were still tuned in, listening for her to close the door, and lock it. Satisfied, once he heard the sounds he was waiting for, he hurried on to his car.

He needed a shower, a shave, and a nap. She wasn't the only one who needed rest.

After she closed the door, she watched through her front window as he drove away. She wished he could've stayed.

But she didn't know him well enough to ask, and she shouldn't be thinking of having his strong arms wrapped around her. Though sleeping with him holding her sounded nice, it wasn't his job to hold her, or to take care of her.

That didn't stop her from longing to be in his arms.

She glanced at the front door. She did feel better with it locked. Deciding to check the back door locks, she headed into the kitchen, and then moved throughout the house, checking all the window locks.

Now that she'd reassured herself she was thoroughly locked in, maybe she'd start to relax.

A hot shower, followed by sweatpants, and a sweatshirt sounded good.

After that, she really did need to call Tanya. By then, it would be late enough on a Sunday that Tanya would be up.

Showered and dressed, Christie poured the last bowl of cereal in the house, and the last of the milk, and then sat on the couch, and looked at the dark screen of the TV. Contemplating turning it on, she decided against it.

Every local channel would be talking about the shooting.

She'd been there, lived through it, and didn't need to listen to the newscasters talking about it repeatedly.

The police had kept the reporters, and their cameras, far from the theater and parking lot, but she'd seen the news vans, camera lights, and reporters hovering, as they waited to pounce.

She needed her life to get back to normal, and to think of things other than the shooter.

Taking a bite of raisin crunch cereal, a remnant of her childhood, she closed her eyes, and forced her thoughts away from the theater, back to when she was ten, and she and Tanya were having a sleepover.

Good memories got her through the cereal, and then she picked up her phone to call her best friend.

She'd have to tell the story again, but she was ready now.

Tanya had always been there for her, and she would be there for her again.

Dialing, she waited for Tanya to answer.

"Christie! Tanya answered the phone right away, as if she'd been waiting for it to ring. "Are you all right?"

Tanya's stress could be felt through the phone line, in her voice.

"I'm okay," Christie said. "It just scared me really bad."

"I bet," Tanya said. "What happened? Where are you now?"

"I'm back home," Christie said.

"Do you want me to come over? I can leave now," Tanya said.

"No, I'm going to try to sleep, after I get off the phone, but thank you," Christie said.

"Okay, if I'm not coming over, I want you to tell me what happened," Tanya said. "tell me everything. My God, I was so worried. I saw it on the news, and they said there'd been a live shooter, and two people were at the hospital, but I called the hospital, and no one would give me any information on them. Then I drove over to the theater, but the police wouldn't let anyone near it."

"I'm so sorry you went through all that stress and worry," Christie said. "They took our cellphones when we went into the theater, and didn't give them back 'til the police let us go. Then I had to get gas on the way home, and it was late, and I was not in a good area."

"The whole night sounds horrible," Tanya said. "I know you're glad to be home. What about the live shooter? Tell me what happened."

Christie knew she'd been dancing around it, talking about everything but that. "We were all watching the movie, everything was normal, except for the cellphone thing, and then this man stood up and just started shooting."

"Oh my God," Tanya said. "What did you do?"

"Well, I was already on the ground, crouching behind my seat, because I'd sat next to a Navy SEAL."

"You what? Sat next to a SEAL? Holy cow," Tanya said. "You got lucky, girl. He was the military guy who stopped the shooter, right?"

"Yes. He saved everyone," Christie said. "He pushed me

down to the ground, before the first shots were fired, and told me to stay down. So, I did what he told me to do."

"Wow. That's incredible! He saved your life."

"Yes, and the lives of everyone in that theater."

"He sounds amazing," Tanya said.

"Oh, he is." Christie curled up on the couch with a throw pillow, and hugged it to herself, thinking how brave he'd been.

Even more of a real movie hero than Cole Kennick.

"He called the police, and then he gave his phone to me, and had me talk to them, while he checked on the wounded."

"Wait," Tanya said. "You said they took all your phones."

"Well, he must've not told them he had one, because he had it on him," Christie said.

"And he had a gun! You're not supposed to have guns in theaters either," Tanya said. "There are signs up."

"I know. He had both," Christie said.

"Oh, he's a rule breaker then. A bad boy," Tanya said.

"I don't know about that," Christie said. "He got along with the police. They didn't even arrest him for having a gun."

"Huh."

"And when he put a tourniquet on the one man, I watched him and listened, and I put one on the other man."

"Wow, really? That means you're a hero, too," Tanya said.

"Oh," Christie felt her cheeks heat at her friend's words.

She hadn't felt particularly heroic.

"I don't know about that. I was just doing what he told me to do. Doing what needed to be done."

"Yeah, I'll bet that's the kind of thing he says too," Tanya said. "Heroes always say that. Unless they have big egos."

Oh. Tanya is right.

"Well, yeah. It is," Christie agreed.

"See?"

But that didn't make her a hero. She wouldn't have even known what to do, if Reed hadn't told her.

Maybe that needed to change.

A man could have bled out right next to her, if Reed hadn't been there with the right tools, and the right instruction.

Do they have classes for that, like they do for CPR?

Another class I really ought to take.

She didn't want to be in a position of standing by helplessly, if there was something she could do to save a life.

5

———

After she ended the call with Tanya, Christie wandered into the kitchen and opened cabinet doors to find something to eat.

She'd planned to stay in, but she really did need to run to the grocery store. That had been on her original "To Do" list for today.

Her stomach growled as she stared at the limited contents of her cabinets.

For the past few weeks, she'd paid for the new dress, the new shoes, and the new purse—basically an entirely new outfit from head to toe. So, she hadn't exactly been buying extras to stock her kitchen. In fact, she'd been eating what she'd already had stored.

Her cabinets held a variety of spices and sauces, pasta with no sauce to put on it, brown rice, pancake syrup, peanut butter, but no bread or crackers, and a yellow cake mix.

She'd had nothing to offer Reed the other night, when he'd escorted her home, except coffee. And it appeared she had little for lunch, or for dinner for herself today.

Last night she hadn't been hungry, but she was paying

for that now, because the small bowl of cereal she'd just eaten for breakfast wasn't enough.

Despite what she'd told Reed about staying in today, she had to go out to buy food.

Taking a small notepad, she started jotting down a quick grocery list, thinking of foods her ex-boyfriend used to like. Salsa and chips, frozen pizza, and mixed nuts. All were good to have on hand to offer a hungry man.

The next time a man came by to visit, she needed to have something on hand to offer him besides coffee.

It had been a year since she'd broken up with Mitch, the last man to sit at her kitchen table until Reed.

She paused, wondering if she was ready to start dating again.

The answer to that question didn't really take much thought. If he was as nice as Reed, she most certainly was.

She wondered if Reed drank alcohol, and if so, what he drank. Her ex drank every night, and many nights he drank a lot. That was one major reason Mitch was an ex. Though he'd been gone a year, she still didn't stock alcohol.

It hadn't been possible to keep drinks in the house when she was with Mitch. He'd finish off anything she brought home.

Over the last few months, she'd bring a bottle of wine home to enjoy, but that was it. Mitch had changed her. Made her wary of enabling someone prone to addictive behaviors.

Now Mitch was gone. It was time to let go of her fear.

She wanted to be prepared the next time she had male company. It wouldn't hurt to have a bottle of wine, if the occasion arose.

Finishing her list, she changed into jeans, and a T-shirt, slipped her feet into her most comfy tennis shoes, and ran a brush through her hair. Glancing in the mirror, she tried to ignore the dark circles.

She needed sleep, but she also needed food, and choosing one meant forgoing the other.

Not until she was behind the wheel of her car, easing into the parking space at the grocery store, did she realize how nervous she was to go out in public again.

The live shooter had changed her view of the world.

She sat in the car, watching people come and go, trying to get her nerve up to get out of the car, and go grocery shopping.

Everything looked calm. Seemed to be staying calm.

Finally, she opened her door, and then got out. After scanning the parking lot again, she headed toward the front doors.

She found herself glancing at faces, trying to read expressions and intent. She'd never been so aware of her surroundings in her life. In fact, she was hyperaware.

Inside the store, she gathered the things she needed, then hurried to check out.

By the time she got home with her purchases, and then carried them into her house, she was exhausted.

Lunch was egg salad on a croissant that she'd picked up at the grocery deli.

She opened the plastic box, and ate her lunch without tasting it, while at the same time, putting everything away.

Afterword, she curled up on the couch, beneath the Afghan that Tanya had made for her. Exhaustion took over, and she fell asleep.

Her cellphone rang, waking her.

She reached for it and squinted to read it.

The house was pitch dark. It was obviously nighttime, and the only light came from her phone.

Tanya's name appeared on the screen.

Christie answered. "Hello?"

"How are you doing?" Tanya asked.

"Okay, I guess," Christie said. "I went to get groceries, ate lunch, and then fell asleep on the couch."

"Oh, did I wake you?" Tanya said, her tone full of regret.

Christie ran a hand over her face, and sat up. "Yes," she said, and then cringed, because she'd sounded a little sharp.

"It's eight o'clock. I wanted to call, before you went to sleep, and make sure you're doing okay. Sorry about waking you."

"It's all right, Tanya, really. I need to get up, and put my pajamas on, and go sleep in my bed, not this old couch." Christie rolled her neck, and stretched. "Thanks for checking on me."

"You're welcome. Is there anything you need?"

"No. I'm all set. I've got to get caught up on sleep, before I go to work tomorrow morning."

"Have you talked to Mrs. Brown? I think you ought to take tomorrow off. You've been through something very traumatic. I'm sure she would understand."

"No, I haven't talked to her," Christie said. "I don't want to take tomorrow off. There's no reason to. I'm fine."

"Okay," Tanya said, sounding doubtful. "Well, call me, if you need anything, or want to talk."

"I'm fine Tanya. Quit fussing." Eager to change the subject, Christie asked. "How are your fur babies?"

"Well, like I texted you, the vet says they ate begonia plants," Tonya said. "It was in the stuff they yakked up."

"I'll bet your awful neighbor is somehow responsible. She planted begonias last month, didn't she?"

"Yeah, but her plants always look great," Tanya said. "She wouldn't allow Miss Priss, or Brutus, in her yard long enough for them to eat them on their own. She hates both of my fur babies. Yells at them to get off her lawn, before one paw even touches her precious grass."

"You need a fence," Christie said.

"Yes, I do." Tanya sighed. "I just don't understand how they both ended up eating the plants. They've never done anything like that before, and for them both to suddenly start that behavior, it seems odd."

"Maybe she poisoned them, somehow," Christie suggested. "Put it in their food."

"How would she do that? She's never been in my house, and she doesn't have a key."

"You think she doesn't. But what if she still has a key, from before you bought the house? Maybe the previous owner gave her a key. If she had one, then she could sneak in while you were away."

Tanya gave a chuckle. "I think that your imagination is running away with you and you need to get more sleep."

"Yeah, I do need sleep. But still, think about it. She could so easily sneak in, if she had a key from before. Did the vet say what begonias do to them? Is it lethal?"

"It makes them throw up, and gives them diarrhea," Tanya said. "But it won't kill them; it just makes them very sick."

"I'm glad they'll be okay now. How are they doing tonight?"

"Fine, just clingy. I had to put Brutus in the other room, and he's in there, whining with his bunny rabbit."

"Poor baby," Christie said. "You know he must still feel bad, if he's whiney, and carrying Wabbit."

Brutus, Tanya's German Shepard, never whined, unless he was sick. Then the big strong guard dog was the biggest baby, and wanted his Wabbit.

Christie loved to go visit, and watch Brutus bark at the mailman, and then turn when the man was gone, and bring her his fluffy pink Wabbit to play with. He could turn off his fierce dog face quick, and then his tail wagged like a happy puppy.

"Maybe I need a dog," she murmured.

"What brought that on? I agree, you should get a dog, and we've had that conversation before," Tanya said. "More times than I can count. Are you feeling lonely? Or scared?"

"No, not lonely," Christie said. "I just think having a good guard dog, like Brutus, would be nice."

"Well, you've got to train dogs," Tanya said. "Let them know you're the alpha. Are you ready to be the alpha?"

"I don't know."

It was an honest answer.

Taking on an alpha role was not something Christie normally did. She didn't like overseeing people.

But, she realized, if you had a dog, you'd have to be in charge, and be the alpha.

Brutus is a big dog. Could I handle a dog that size?

"I've pictured you more with a lap dog," Tanya said. "You get the cuddling, as well as the guarding then."

Christie chewed on her lower lip, as she thought about that.

"Yeah, but if there's a prowler, a German Shepard would be better protection."

"True. Look, if you're serious, I can take you to where I found Brutus," Tanya said. "You can talk to them about their next litter."

"Yeah, I might want to do that," Christie agreed.

"All right. You get some sleep, and we'll talk about it later this week. I'll call them to see about a visit."

"Okay. Thanks, Tanya."

"Night, girlfriend. I'm real glad you're still here to talk to. You'll always be my bestie. I love you."

Christie smiled. "Love you, too." Tanya was her oldest, and best friend. It felt good to be loved, and appreciated. She didn't know what she'd do without Tanya either. "I'm glad you called."

"Me, too."

"I'll call you after work tomorrow," Christie said.

"Sounds good," Tanya said.

"Good night," Christie said.

"Good night, bestie," Tanya said.

They both hung up, and Christie sat for a moment, smiling, and thinking how lucky she was to have Tanya in her life.

Christie had a job she loved, a home that was finally decorated just the way she'd always wanted, and a great best friend. Now, she just needed a dog companion, to cuddle with, and to scare away bad guys.

Life was good, and it was good to be alive. But it was awfully quiet here.

Tanya was right. Sometimes, Christie did get lonely.

Maybe I'll look at dogs this week. Then I'll have companionship, and be safer.

M onday morning came like every other Monday morning, yet not.

This one came with the happy realization she'd be working with the flowers she loved so much, a thought she had every workday morning. But this time she had a new thought added.

What if some crazy person comes into the florist shop, and starts waving a gun around, or worse, starts shooting?

This was something she'd never thought of before, and the realization that a live shooter could pop up anywhere shook her comfortable familiar world.

There was no going back.

No way to return to innocence, and the days of thinking everyone coming into the store was a nice man, or woman.

There were crazy, bad people in the world, and they'd pop up when you least expected it. When you weren't ready. When you didn't know what to do.

If there was a fire, she knew what to do.

If someone tried to rob the store, she knew what to do. She'd hand over the money, and hope that no one got hurt.

But a crazy person, someone who wants to kill people? Who wants to shoot them in cold blood?

That she wasn't prepared for.

She felt different now. Changed.

Now, she expected violence. Knew it could happen. No longer did she live with a naïve mindset that believed nothing like that would ever happen to her, or to anyone she knew.

Because now, it had.

She didn't know what to do with all these new thoughts, and feelings. The shooting had happened, and now she didn't know how to be.

Her life now fell into a split of what had happened before the live shooter, and what had happened after.

But the "after" part of her life story wasn't written yet, and she was standing on the page, not quite knowing what to do.

At least she'd slept last night, but her sleep had been restless. She knew she'd dreamed, but couldn't remember what the dream was about.

Which was likely just as well.

She had enough dealing with what was going through her head in her awake moments, without adding in the dreamtime thoughts, too.

Usually on her way to work, she'd turn on the radio, and listen to music she liked, and sometimes she even sang along. But today, she didn't even turn the radio on.

No radio, like no TV, meant no news.

It meant she wouldn't have to hear them talk about the shooting.

She drove in silence, until she pulled into her parking place, behind the shop, and then sat in the car for a few minutes, before turning it off.

Everything was quiet.

In the car, and outside of the car.

It was early. She usually came in an hour before they opened to the public, to start working on the arrangements needed for the week's orders.

The silence in the car was a new thing, and a needed thing.

She opened the door, took her keys out of the car, and then walked to the back door. Unlocking it, she cracked the door, and peered inside, before pushing it open all the way.

All was quiet. She was the only one here.

Good.

She pushed the door the rest of the way open, and walked into the shop, quickly locking the door behind her.

No one can get in, while both doors are locked.

For the first hour, the shop remained quiet, as she worked on a silver arrangement, with blue and purple flowers, for the grand opening of a new hair salon.

When that was done, she made three red rose arrangements for wedding anniversaries, and one pink rosebud arrangement for a sweet sixteen birthday.

The hour went by fast, and she'd just finished the arrangements, when Mrs. Brown opened the front door.

"Good morning," she breezed in, with her usual pep, past Christie and the beautiful arrangements standing on the long table. "Oh, these are lovely."

"Thank you," Christie quietly answered.

Mrs. Brown, always quite perceptive, slowed down to a

stop, to look at Christie more closely. "Something has happened."

"Yes," Christie replied.

Mrs. Brown's kind and concerned blue eyes watched her.

Like a sweet, caring grandmother, she was easy to talk to.

Christie's hands dropped to her sides. "You probably heard the news... ' She took a deep breath. "That theater shooting. I was there. Inside the theater, watching that movie."

"Oh, Christie, no!" Mrs. Brown gasped. "Oh, I'm so glad you're all right." She reached for Christie's arm. "Come over here, and sit down."

Taking her by the elbow, she moved Christie toward the small table and two chairs, in the corner of the room, where they took their breaks and meals.

Christie let herself be guided, and once they both sat, she said, "It was frightening."

"Why, yes, my dear girl, that would have been," Mrs. Brown nodded, as she patted Christie's hand. "Terribly frightening. Now, tell me what happened."

Christie blew out a deep breath, before starting to share her story. "We were just sitting there, watching the movie, when this crazy man came in with a gun, and started shooting."

Mrs. Brown nodded. "I saw on the news it had happened, but they didn't name any of the theater patrons."

"No,' Christie shook her head. "I believe they'll keep our names private."

"That's good," Mrs. Brown said. "You don't need reporters pestering you. What happened with the Navy SEAL? I heard that he saved everyone."

"He did," Christie nodded vigorously. "He stopped the shooter, shot him, and then he helped two wounded men who'd been shot. I helped him."

"You did?" Mrs. Brown's eyes widened with surprise.

"I did." Christie nodded. "Put a tourniquet on, and everything."

Mrs. Brown gave her hand a squeeze. "Christie, I'm so proud of you. I didn't know you had any sort of medical training."

"I don't, but Reed talked me through it."

"Reed." Mrs. Brown smiled. "What a nice name. He sounds like quite the hero. Is he very handsome?"

"Oh, yes, very," Christie said, and felt a blush suffuse her cheeks.

"Built, too, I'll wager," Mrs. Brown said, arching one eyebrow.

"Oh, yes. Very built." Christie nodded, remembering the way his muscles flexed, when he moved. The power he held in his body.

"Very handsome, built, and a hero. A Navy SEAL," Mrs. Brown said. "Yes, he would be. Is he married?"

"No. I don't think so." Christie shook her head. "I didn't see a ring."

Ever the romantic, her employer held a hand to her heart. "I think this was meant to be. Not just chance that brought you two together."

Christie shrugged. "Maybe."

"It's time you started dating," the older woman nodded.

"Well, he hasn't asked me," Christie said. "And I may never see him again."

"I wouldn't be so sure. When it's fated, there is always a way." Mrs. Brown winked.

～

Tuesday passed quietly, much like Monday, but on Wednesday, when the bell over the door of the shop jingled, and Christie looked up from watering the flowers near the front of the store, she saw Reed entering the florist shop.

"Hello," she said, with surprise, her heart suddenly skittering faster.

"Hello, Christie," he said with a smile. "How are you doing?"

"I'm good. Been working with my flowers." She beamed at him. "I'm glad you found the shop. Are you here to place an order, or pick up a bouquet? We have some lovely ones today."

"Actually..." He stepped closer, until he was standing near enough to touch, his gaze never leaving hers. "I came in looking for you."

Christie blushed, and dipped her head, feeling the heat rise in her neck, and cheeks. "You did?"

"I did," he said. "I thought I'd invite you to the range, for date night, if you're interested."

He'd come in looking for her, to ask her out.

She wanted to pinch herself.

Wait. Date night. Range?

She squeaked out the last word, before she realized she'd spoken out loud.

"Yes, the gun range," he said. "They have a couples' date night. We'd be able to shoot, and have dinner there. Saturday night, if you'd like to go."

The concept was boggling her mind.

People do this. This is a date thing.

"This Saturday," he said. "If you're free."

Oh, he keeps talking, because I haven't answered him.

He was waiting for an answer.

Her mind was in a spin. "I-I've never been to a gun range," she said. "I don't know anything about guns."

"That part's easy," he said, "I'll teach you."

"Teach me to shoot guns?" Her voice was doing that squeaking thing again.

Oh, why can't I answer him normally, without sounding like a frightened little mouse?

His lips twitched. "Yes, teach you to shoot guns. You can learn to shoot handguns, or long guns, if you like rifles better. Anything you want to start with."

"Oh. Wow." Her eyes wide, she tried to wrap her head around the idea of this handsome Navy SEAL teaching her how to shoot guns. Images of old western movies where the hero taught the heroine how to shoot guns flooded into her head.

The hero would put his arms around the heroine, to show her how to shoot, and he'd be so close.

Reed would be so close.

Longing wrestled with fear, a long-standing fear of guns.

She stood silent while they wrestled.

6

———

Reed watched the range of emotions, that slid across Christie's face, like a continually changing kaleidoscope, a mesmerizing show, that had begun, the moment she'd noticed him walking through the door.

Quite simply, she fascinated him.

Clearly, she was entertaining many new thoughts.

He'd have to try harder to convince her.

"The dinner special Saturday night, is meatloaf, mashed potatoes, and green beans. It's country-style food there, and they usually have a few fresh pies to choose from for dessert. So, wear jeans, a comfortable shirt, closed-toe shoes, and bring your appetite." He gave her his warmest smile. "Sound like fun?"

She blinked. "Yes."

"Good. I can pick you up after work. You pick the time, and I'll make the arrangements," he said.

"Oh, okay, yes. Well," she said. "I usually get off work at five on Saturdays."

A short, white-haired lady, who must've been the Mrs. Brown Christie had spoken of, poked her head out of the back room. "You'll be off at four on Saturday, my dear. Plenty of time to go shooting."

Surprised, Christie swung her head to look at Mrs. Brown. "An hour early?"

"Don't think I haven't noticed more than a bit of overtime happening lately, my dear, which hasn't shown up on your time sheet," Mrs. Brown said. "And we don't have any big orders to work on, until next week."

"Oh, all right then. Thank you, Mrs. Brown." Christie smiled at her.

"You're welcome, dear," Mrs. Brown said cheerily.

"Oh!" Christie turned back toward Reed. "I haven't introduced you. Reed Tindal this is Mrs. Brown. Mrs. Brown, this is Mr. Tindal."

"Nice to meet you," Mrs. Brown said.

"Pleased to meet you as well," Reed said.

"Well, since I'm off early," Christie said. "You can pick me up at five—if that's not too soon—or five thirty."

"Not too soon. That's perfect," he said.

He smiled his thanks at Mrs. Brown.

She winked at him, and ducked away into the back room again.

"I'll pick you up at five," he said.

"I'm looking forward to it," Christie said.

Reed scanned the colorful flowers, wondering which she would like best and said, "Which is your favorite? Roses?"

Every woman likes red roses.

"It's hard for me to choose," she replied. "There's a language of flowers, you know."

"There is? I didn't know that." He watched her, thinking, *she's full of surprises, and things to learn.*

"It can be complicated," she said. "But I could teach you." A blush spread across her cheeks at that.

He tilted his head. "Sounds fair. I'll teach you how to shoot, and you teach me the language of flowers."

"It's a deal," she said softly, blushing even deeper.

"But if you had to pick a favorite flower, today?"

"Today, I would pick lilies," she pointed to a selection of lilies in various colors. "White lilies, with some greenery, and babies' breath."

He nodded. "Very pretty."

"I'm making an arrangement for a twenty-fifth wedding anniversary tomorrow," she said. "White lilies, and baby's breath. They're having a dinner party, and a pianist."

"Sounds elegant."

"Oh, yes," she smiled. "Very elegant. I'm looking forward to doing their arrangement."

"You love your job."

"Yes, I do." She nodded.

It's a nice change, to meet a woman who loves her job. One who is happy with her life. A nice change of pace.

"I should let you get back to work," he said, surprised by how reluctant he felt leaving her. "I'll see you Saturday."

Her smile was wide and sweet. "Yes! See you Saturday."

He let himself out the door, the image of Christie surrounded by a profusion of colorful flowers staying with him.

~

Christie moved restlessly about her kitchen, watching the clock.

Reed would arrive in twenty minutes, and then they were going shooting.

She still couldn't believe she was going to a gun range.

Reed was the only person who could have talked her into it. Though that's not how it had happened.

59

She'd said yes so fast, she couldn't exactly remember how it had happened. Now, she was going to a gun range, to learn how to shoot.

I wonder if he makes a habit of taking women on first dates to the gun range. It certainly is an unusual way to start a dating relationship.

She ran her hands down her best jeans, and fussed with her new T-shirt.

Tuck the shirt in or wear it out?

Tucking it in, showed off her figure. Wearing it out, was more comfortable.

She opted for out.

The T-shirt was pale pink, and decorated with embroidered purple violets, with the saying, *Flowers are my superpower*, beneath.

Absentmindedly, she checked her fridge and freezer, again. This time, she had a frozen pizza, chips, popcorn, colas, and a bottle of red wine. Much more than coffee to offer him, if they ended up back at her house, hanging out.

Though this date did include dinner, and they might not end up here afterward, or be hungry if they did.

At least she was now prepared for a man's visit, and could offer him something besides coffee.

Reed rang the doorbell, and she hurried to the door.

She opened it to see his smiling face looking down on her.

He read her T-shirt. "Nice shirt. It suits you."

"Thank you," she said. She took him in, from head to toe.

His tanned face, dark hair, along with a smile, which reached his eyes. Broad shoulders beneath a plain brown t-shirt, and his leather jacket, and blue jeans showed his toned and muscular physique in a sexy yet understated way.

"You look nice too."

"Are you ready?" he asked.

"As ready as I can be," she said.

She grabbed her purse, and then stepped outside her house, and locked the door.

"Nervous after the shooting?" he asked.

"Yes," she said. "Very nervous."

Placing his hand on the small of her back, to guide her to his car, he said, "I'll have to see what I can do, to ease your fears. Were you afraid of guns before the theater shooting?"

"Yes, I was," she nodded.

He opened the car door for her, and said, "Have you ever been around guns? Maybe growing up?"

"I'll tell you about it on the way," she said.

"Sounds good." He closed her door, and went over to the driver's side, opened the door, and got in.

After starting the car, he turned the radio off, and turned his full attention to Christie.

She sighed, and then began to tell him. "My dad used to hunt," she said. "And he had guns. Shotguns, and rifles. I can remember them being in a large wooden case, with glass doors, that mother and daddy kept locked. So, in a way, I was around guns. But I was always told not to touch them."

"And when you got older?"

"Daddy died in a car accident when I was ten. He was in his truck on the highway. A semi went out of control, and daddy didn't live long after he was hit."

"Sorry to hear that." Reed's face showed concern. "That had to be hard, losing a father so young."

"It was. Mother did something with his guns." She shook her head. "I'm not sure what, but they went away, and I never saw them again. Mother remarried, but my stepdad didn't shoot, or go hunting. He's a businessman, and he works, and golfs."

"I see." Reed glanced at her, before looking back to the road.

He was a good driver, and made her feel safe. But then his very presence did that.

"So, for you," he said, "Guns were big, scary no-noes."

"Right."

"And you still see guns from a child's point of view."

She wrinkled her nose. "Probably."

"Did you ever see your dad handling the guns? Loading them, or cleaning them?"

"Once, he had them on the kitchen table, cleaning them. He'd started to show me what he was doing, but mother returned from buying groceries, freaked out, and told me I wasn't ever to touch them, and to leave the room."

"So, you've picked up your mother's fear of guns," he said. "They wouldn't have hurt you, because he would have had to unload them, to clean them."

She nodded. "Yes, he said they were unloaded. They argued about it, and I heard him tell her that."

"Okay. I'm going to start you off, with learning the parts of a gun. I'll show you a shotgun, a rifle, and two handguns —a revolver, and a nine-millimeter. I'll show you how the guns are put together, and how they work. Somewhat like what your dad was trying to teach you, before your mother walked in."

"That would be great. He did want me to learn about them." She smiled. "I think he'd approve of this part of our date."

He raised an eyebrow. "Good, but let's not get into the habit of bringing along what your daddy would approve of, on our dates. That could get uncomfortable."

She laughed. "Oh yeah, it could."

"I'd have had the father and teenage-boy talk, if I'd dated you in high school, I'll wager," he said.

"Oh yeah, you would've." She agreed. "Daddy was real protective. My stepdad? Not so much. With him, it's all about the money. How much a dress for the prom would cost. I always felt like he saw me as a burden. He didn't like paying for someone else's daughter."

"Are he and your mother still married?" he asked.

"Yeah. They still live in Pennsylvania, so I don't see them much. I stopped going to visit, after they never came here. I mean, the 'it's too expensive, and too far' works both ways. But I still call mother, once a week. That's what works best, for everyone. He keeps her real busy."

"So, you get along, you just don't see each other."

"Something like that," she said. "I have real good memories of my dad, and we were close. It wasn't like I needed a new dad. Sometimes, I miss him, and start getting sad, but then I remember how he always hated to see me, or mother sad, and he'd say something to cheer us up. So, I remember those things until I'm not so sad anymore. And it's gotten better with time."

"I hear you. Grief isn't an easy thing at any age. Sounds like you learned how to deal with it young."

"Yes" she said. "I did."

"I've lost family members, and I've lost men on my team who were like brothers. It's never easy, but we can't let it pull us down. We have to keep living. That's what they'd want us to do."

"Yes. We do," she agreed. "I'm glad we're going shooting today."

And she was. Somehow, he'd taken her fear, and by talking about it, had made it a faceable and beatable thing.

He's so easy to talk to.

That was rare, and even rarer in someone she'd just met.

When they reached the shooting range, he parked the car, and then got out, to come around and open her door.

The range was a long, one-story building with a sign on the front, stating the name, with no other decoration. There was some greenery by the front door entrance, but that was it.

She'd never have guessed there was a restaurant inside.

He opened the door for her, and she got out. Then he went to the trunk and opened it.

Inside were two long gun cases, which he pulled out, before closing the lid. "I brought a shot gun, a rifle, and two handguns. We'll have to let them check the guns, once we enter, and then I can show you how they work, before we go onto the range."

"Okay." She'd be doing far more than she'd thought she'd be doing when she agreed to this guns and dinner date. And she wasn't sure she'd remember everything, after being introduced to so many kinds of guns, but so far, it sounded all right.

Reed was making it easy for her, and she was comfortable around him, if not the guns.

They walked inside, and over to the counter.

The man working the counter asked for their IDs, and for them to sign a sheet. He had to put her into the computer, since she'd never been there, but Reed had been, many times.

Once they'd registered, and Reed had paid for the dinner date, they headed toward a room in the back.

Inside the room were picnic-style tables, and the room looked onto the firing range, which they could see and hear through a glass window. It was loud, busy, and smelled funny.

In sensory overload, Christie's nerves were on high alert.

Bang.

Christie jumped.

Bang.

She jumped again.

Bang.

With each bang, she jumped, and now, she cringed and wanted to cover her head. She sank onto the picnic table seat to do just that, dropping the targets ,and the ammo onto the table.

Her hands went up over her ears. Her arms curving over herself protectively.

Bangs and pops kept coming, just like in the theater.

She huddled on the picnic table seat, like a frightened mouse. Not aware of anything else, but her fear, and the noises of the guns, her heart raced. Her thoughts raced.

Oh my God, oh my God, oh my God.

7

———

Shit. Reed's heart sank when he saw her reaction to the noise of the guns.

What the hell was I thinking? Bringing her here. I should've predicted this. Maybe this isn't the best idea. I thought she'd be okay.

He was on the other side of the table with the guns, but he quickly placed them on the table, and moved around to her side.

Sitting beside her, he put his arms around her, and said, "Christie, hey, it's me, Reed. You're okay. We're just at the range. Nobody is going to hurt you. It's safe here. I got you."

He kept his voice calm, knowing he needed to help her realize where she was, and that she was safe, before this got any worse.

Then he heard her small whisper. "Reed?"

"Yes, sweetheart. I'm here. You're safe. We're sitting on the picnic table, at the range."

"I know."

Good. She hasn't drifted. She knows where she is.

"You know you're safe, right? I wouldn't let anything happen to you."

She nodded.

Affirmative. Good.

"I was going to take these guns apart, and show you how they work, remember?"

"Yes."

He waited to see what she'd do next. He stayed quiet, not asking her yet, if she wanted to continue.

Finally, she raised her head, and he pulled back a little, still holding her in his arms.

She looked up at him, and blinked twice.

Her face was pale, with none of the blushing color he'd seen before.

He saw tears starting to form.

"I'm sorry I'm such a big baby," she said. "I'm ruining our date."

"Naw. You're not a baby," he said. "You're a woman. And you're not ruining anything."

She sat up a little taller, and sniffled. "Okay, if you say so." She shrugged. "I'll watch, if you still want to show me."

"Of course, I do." His tone brushed that off, in a 'don't be silly' kind of way, and then he stood again, to refocus her attention on his guns.

"Okay, so we'll go over the rifle first, then the shotgun, and then the handguns. We'll start with the kinds of guns your daddy used."

She smiled at him, probably remembering her daddy. "Okay."

He showed her his guns, talked to her about them, and asked about her dads' guns, and about her dad, until she finally started to relax.

"Thank you," she said and he noted how the color had once again come back into her cheeks.

"You brought memories of my dad that I'd long forgotten, back to me, and I've learned a lot about guns today."

"You're welcome," he said. "Now, I'll let you shoot them. First, we'll start with the rifle. I'll have you try each gun, at least once, and then we'll figure out what you like to shoot."

"Okay," she agreed.

"When we go onto the range to shoot, we'll wear ear protection and eye protection," Reed said. "You can tell from here how loud it gets in there."

"Oh, yes," she said. "It is loud, even through the glass, before we have to put on ear protection."

He unzipped one of the cases, and took out a shotgun. "We'll start with this one. Have a seat."

She sat at the table and watched, as he took the shotgun apart. Once apart, he put it back together, naming the parts, and showing her how the gun worked.

He repeated this process with the rifle, the revolver, and the nine-millimeter. By the time he was done, she was no longer afraid of the guns, like she had been, before they started.

As she watched him pick the guns up, to carry them into the range where they would shoot, thoughts ran through her head.

Guns are nothing without bullets. With them, they're lethal. Without, they're like a car without gas. Nice to look at, but useless without what it takes to make them go.

"Okay, you carry the targets and the ammo," he said. "I've got the rest."

She picked up the paper targets, and boxes of ammo, and followed him.

Before they entered the range, he made sure she donned eye, and ear protection, and then motioned for her to follow him.

He spoke to the range master, and then headed toward number four lane, where he placed the handguns on a small table, along with the long guns.

He raised his voice, so she could hear, and said, "Put the ammo here, and hand me the targets."

She put the ammo down, and handed over the targets.

He pushed a button, and a metal piece connected to a track in the ceiling sped the metal piece toward them, until it stopped right in front of him. Then he attached the paper target with the picture of a man pointing a gun at them.

Finally, he pushed the button again, and it sped back to twenty yards where he stopped it.

He showed her how to shoot the shotgun, and then it was her turn to shoot.

Placing it high against her right shoulder, she put her cheek next to the gun, like he'd told her to, and then lined up the target, and squeezed the trigger.

The gun pulled up as she shot, and her shot went wide up, and to the right.

"I missed him," she said. "The gun jumped."

"You jumped," he said. "That's typical with new shooters. They jump. It's not the gun."

"I don't like this one," she said, rubbing her shoulder. "It's too much."

He eyed her small shoulders, and nodded. "You don't have to shoot that one, if you don't want to. Or you can finish out the bullets. Then we'll move on to the next one."

"I don't want to shoot that one anymore," she said. "It hurts me."

"Okay, I'll shoot." He reached for the shotgun, and she gladly gave it to him.

She watched, as he fired off the rest of the shots, each one making a bull's-eye, all shots right through the hole the first shot had made.

"Wow," she said. "Do you ever miss?"

"Yeah," he said. "I'm not perfect. So, I do miss. But not

with a shotgun, and not at twenty yards. If I miss this close, someone might die."

She scrunched her nose. "This probably seems like nothing to you. Easy as child's play."

"It's not nothing," he said. "I enjoy shooting. And I'm enjoying teaching you. Next up, the rifle."

She eyed it. "Is that one going to hurt my shoulder too?"

"No," he shook his head. "This one doesn't have the recoil that shotguns have."

She tried it, and found that she enjoyed shooting the rifle. It reminded her of her dad's rifle.

Her dad had gone shooting nearly every weekend. She wished she'd been allowed to go with him, even once.

"On to handguns," Reed said. "Which one do you want to shoot first?"

"The revolver," she said. "It looks like those guns in the wild west."

"It is," he said. "These are fun guns to shoot. First though, do you remember how to load it?"

"Yes," she nodded.

"Okay," he said. "Go ahead and load."

She loaded six shots into the revolver, and then looked at him expectantly.

"Now, go ahead and shoot," he said. "Just the way I showed you."

"Okay." She stepped up, and aimed. Then she fired.

This time this gun only jumped a little.

She glanced over her shoulder at Reed.

"Hold on," he said.

She waited, while he corrected her position, moving her fingers.

"Try to relax. You've got a death grip going on. And remember to breathe. You're stressing too much."

"Yeah," she admitted. "A little."

She fired the gun again, and something hot, flew up, and landed on her head, making her jump.

Christie laid the gun down on the table, and touched her head with her hand, feeling where the hot thing had landed on her. She looked at Reed.

"It's just a shell casing," he said. "Sometimes they do that."

She glanced down at the ground, where shell casings lay.

"It was hot," she said.

"Yes," he said. "But it didn't hurt you."

She gave him a nod. It hadn't hurt her.

Just startled her, scaring her enough to make her jump.

Reed pushed the button, and the metal thing holding the target came sliding back to him. He unclipped the paper, and then handed it to her, so she could see her shots close.

"Good job for your first-time shooting," Reed said, encouraging approval in his voice.

"I did okay?" She wasn't so sure.

Some shots had gone wide of the target, not even hitting it, while others had hit the target, but not in the center.

She was showing her insecurities, but she didn't care. She was just being herself, which was so easy with him.

"For your first time shooting a gun, you did," he said. "More than okay. Did you enjoy yourself?"

She thought for a minute, trying to decide if she'd enjoyed herself.

He'd made it easy for her. Being with him was easy.

"Yes," she said, surprised the answer was true.

"Good," he said. "I'm hungry. You ready to eat?"

"Yes." That, she had an answer for right away. She was hungrier than she'd thought she'd be.

"Okay," he said. "Let's go." He picked up the guns, and she held the targets, and picked up the remaining ammo.

Once outside the range, they removed their eye and ear protection, and then he put the guns in their cases.

"Okay, before we eat, you'll want to wash your hands." He glanced down hers. "Gunpowder. They've got a special soap for that."

"Oh!" she said. "Yes, I'd like to freshen up."

"We passed the restrooms on the way in. I'm going to put these back in the trunk, and then I'll meet you in the waiting area."

"Okay." The waiting area she'd seen, had leather couches, and that must be where he meant. "I'll wait for you there."

She entered the ladies' room, washed her hands, then used the facilities, and washed her hands again.

She wasn't sure if she smelled like gunpowder, or if the scent was only in her nose, but the soap in the ladies' room had a nice scent, so that helped.

How does one remain pretty, and sweet-smelling, when on a date at the gun range? The soap, I guess. I like to smell good when I'm on dates. But maybe that isn't as important to men as I thought it was.

Christie thought about the primping she'd done after work, to get ready for her informal jeans and T-shirt date, and laughed to herself.

He probably didn't even notice. His mind is on the guns.

Coming out of the ladies' room, and around the corner to where the waiting area was, she saw Reed already standing ,and waiting for her.

Had she taken that long? Or was he just fast.

He gave her a wide smile, and then placing his warm hand at the small of her back, escorted her into the restaurant.

It was an informal, 'seat yourselves' kind of restaurant, and it was getting busy.

He sat them at one of two tables left.

"Does the special sound good to you, or would you like to see the menu?" he asked, pointing at the blackboard.

"Oh, I'm fine with the special. I like good old-fashioned foods, like meatloaf, and mashed potatoes."

"Great!" He signaled for the waitress, who came over with pen and pad.

"Ready to order?" she asked.

"Yes, ma'am. We'll both have the special," he said.

"And to drink?"

"What do you have?" Christie asked. Maybe she'd need that menu after all.

The waitress rattled off a list of soft drinks, until she hit one that sounded good to Christie.

"Root beer," she said. "I haven't had that in a long time."

"Good choice. It's from a local bottling company," the waitress said. "Everyone likes it."

"I'll have tea, unsweetened, and bring sugar," Reed said.

"You're a sweet tea drinker," Christie said.

"Texas, born and raised. We drank it like water down there, with nearly every meal," he said.

"Oh, that makes sense," Christie said.

"So, Christie," he said, leaning back in his chair. "How did you like shooting those four guns, for the first time?"

"I didn't like the shotgun," she shook her head hard, "because it hurt my shoulder, but I do like the twenty-two."

"Those are fun guns to shoot. Lots of kids start out shooting twenty-twos with their dads, when they're young."

"So, it's more of a child's gun," she said. "Not really a useful gun?"

"No, it's just an easy gun to learn. And if you're good with it, you could shoot rabbits, and other small game. So, it can be useful. For an intruder though, reach for a shotgun over a twenty-two. More stopping power."

"I don't think I want a shotgun," she said.

"For home protection, I'd suggest a handgun over a shotgun, for you. And you can carry a handgun, but you can't go walking down the street with a shotgun. A handgun is the first gun you should buy."

"I'm not ready to buy a gun," she said, shaking her head.

"Of course not. It's too soon," he said. "No one here is going to pressure you to buy a gun. But what did you think of the handguns? Do you have a preference?"

"I liked the revolver, at first," she said. "But I didn't like the hot bullet part landing on my head!"

"I can understand that" he said. "Bullet casings can be hot. That wasn't the good first experience I'd hoped for you."

"Do you have a lot of guns?" she asked.

"Heh." He grinned sheepishly. "To a civilian, the answer would be yes."

"And to your Navy SEAL buddies?"

"Not as many as some. More than others," he said. "Though I have a knife collection some of them drool over."

"Wow. So, you collect guns and knives."

"Guns, knives, tactical flashlights."

"Flashlights?"

"Yeah. And that's a thing we can get you now, whether you decide to buy a gun or not. A good tactical flashlight is a thing everyone should carry." He reached and pulled a black, heavy-looking flashlight off of his belt. "I can show you what it can do, once it's dark, but this is what I carry."

She looked at the flashlight but made no move toward it.

"It won't hurt you," he laughed. "You're not in a James Bond movie. It does what it does, no Hollywood spy stuff added. Though it's very versatile, if you know what to do with it."

She picked it up. "It's heavy."

"Yep." He watched her wrap her hand around it, and grinned.

"Do you know what you've got there?" he asked.

She started to let loose, but his hand wrapped around hers, holding her fingers closed around the flashlight, as he leaned in, to speak quietly to her.

"Like brass knuckles, you hit a guy while holding that flashlight, like this, it's going to hurt. Far more than your soft hand would."

"Oh!" His warm, strong hand holding hers, and her thoughts moving into a more intimate range now, had her flustered.

His mind isn't on that; it's on me, fighting to defend myself! Get your mind out of the gutter, Christie. He's trying to help you!

She blushed an even deeper red.

Thankfully, her root beer came.

She put down the flashlight, and reached for her drink.

Their food came soon after.

She looked at the large helping of meatloaf, and mashed potatoes, with the little bowl of green beans on the side.

"Hearty country food. What did I tell you?" Reed said.

"Yes, it sure is," she said. "Looks good."

"But save room for pie," he said. "They have apple, and pecan tonight."

"I'll be wanting apple," she said. "Of the two, I like it the best."

"That's my favorite, too," he said.

"My favorite is blueberry, but apple runs a close second."

"That's a good one, too," he said.

She nodded. Hungrier than she'd thought she'd be, she dug into her mashed potatoes. "These are one of my comfort foods," she said. "When I've had a bad day, or I'm not feeling so good, I like mashed potatoes."

"With gravy?" he asked.

"Yes, unless my stomach is upset," she nodded. "Then I just eat them plain."

"I don't have a comfort food," he said. "I mostly eat to fuel my body, unless I'm hungry for something in particular."

"Wow," Christie said. "I keep chocolate on hand, for when I'm stressed. But at the theater the other night, I didn't crave it. Usually I do."

"That was an extreme situation," Reed said.

"It was," she agreed. "I'm sorry about my reaction to the loud guns in the shooting room."

"On the range," he corrected her. "And don't be sorry. You got through it okay, and it will get easier."

"I quit watching TV," she said. "The live shooter was all they wanted to talk about."

She'd stopped watching the news, after the live shooter incident, exhausted by having to listen to the story over, and over.

There was never anything good on the news, and who needed all that negativity?

"I never watched it much to begin with," he said. "The reporting is not always accurate."

"I just can't handle it anymore," she said. "I'm going to start listening to music instead."

"What kind of music do you like?" he said.

"Oh, jazz, swing, big band, old time country." She grinned at him. "I like old music, old cars, and vintage anything."

"Sounds interesting," he said. "You'll have to share your music with me some time."

"I'd like that," she said.

As they ate, she asked about Navy SEAL training.

He explained many of the things he'd had to do to reach his current rank and skills.

Mostly, she listened, fascinated by it all.

She was on a date with an honest to God Navy SEAL, and he was talking to her, as if he were just another guy, describing his day at work.

It left her in awe. She couldn't help it. She'd never met a Navy SEAL before Reed.

Reed didn't miss how rapt she was over every word he spoke, about his SEAL training, and anything to do with the SEALs. He was used to that, but hoped she wouldn't go into a state of hero worship, where she didn't see him as Reed, the man. He hoped that, with time, she'd reach that point as they continued dating.

Over pie, Reed brought up the question he'd been deciding all night whether to ask her.

He liked Christie, a lot. But he'd wanted to get to know her better, before asking her out again.

Christie was the first girly-girl he'd dated. He hadn't expected her to take to the guns, wanting to shoot every-thing, and to be excited about all of them, like his other girl-friends.

She didn't have enough tomboy in her to do that. But he hoped she'd at least enjoyed shooting one of the guns, so they could go to the range occasionally, and she could learn how to protect herself.

It seemed like she had.

Maybe this could work, the two of them. Opposites did attract. And they were opposites.

But beyond attraction, could they stick?

He needed a woman who could be a team player, who could be a partner, not just a pretty face who was good in bed. And it wasn't easy being with a SEAL.

SEALs could be called away any minute, with no notice, and might not be able to tell their women where they were going, or even after they got back, where they went.

It took a special kind of woman to be with a SEAL, long-term.

He'd thought he'd found that once. But she couldn't keep her pants on, when he was out of town, and had run off with some other dude. Breaking it off with no explanation.

Christie, though, was like no woman he'd ever known. She intrigued him, and he enjoyed her company.

Not to mention the chemistry between them, which he'd had to ignore tonight, so he could focus on the guns, and on teaching her. Maybe it wasn't the most romantic date, but he would make that up to her.

He had a plan.

They'd been thrown together, might never have met otherwise, and maybe there was a little bit of good luck, and a little bit of fate in that.

Whatever it was, he wasn't going to examine it too closely.

He'd enjoy her company, keep getting to know her, and see where it went.

Now, it was time to plunge in, and ask her out again. This time, there'd be romance.

"In two weeks, my best friend, R.T., is getting married," he said. "And I'm in the wedding party. I don't have a date yet. Would you like to go?"

Christie watched his face, stunned.

Reed held his breath.

Was this date too much for her? Am I too much for her?

Maybe she can't handle dating a SEAL.

Will she say no?

8

———————

Christie sat stunned.

Two weeks until the wedding, and Reed said he doesn't have a date yet.

Does that mean he isn't dating anyone else, right now?

"Yes, I'd love to go." She tried to answer quickly, to make up for the time lapse after being stunned.

This was moving fast, she and Reed.

"Excellent." Reed smiled.

He drove her home, thinking of how much he was looking forward to kissing her.

Finally, they were at her front door, and he was watching her use her key in the lock.

When she stopped, and looked up at him, he moved in, bending down to kiss her.

His lips met hers, in a gentle, testing way.

She responded, sweet, and letting him take the lead.

His tongue teased her lips, until they opened, letting him in. Their tongues touched, and it was electric.

Their chemistry was off the charts, as they explored each other, and she was both sweet, and eager.

He could have kissed her all night, but it was a first date, and he could tell she was an old-fashioned kind of girl, with traditional values.

As he pulled away, his gaze met hers.

She smiled. "I had a good time tonight," she said.

"I did too," he said. "If you enjoyed going to the range, we'll have to do it again."

"I did enjoy it," she said. "And I would like that."

He made sure she was inside her house, with the door locked, before he walked back to his car.

Now that Reed had a date for the wedding, he needed to get on over to Chicks Oyster Bar and Marina, where the grooms meeting for the wedding was taking place.

Most of the guys were already there, when Reed arrived.

Diesel waved him over. "Hey man, glad you could make it," he said, with a grin.

It was clear he was excited about the wedding.

"Wouldn't miss it," Reed said. "Just had to stop by, and ask a lady to be my date."

"She say yes?" Cutter asked.

Reed just gave him a look.

"Of course, she did," Kik laughed.

Since Cutter was waiting for an answer, Reed nodded.

Cutter laughed.

All the men were in good spirits, and enjoying a draft beer. Diesel's treat.

Sheri, their waitress, paused beside Reed, and said, "What are you having?"

"A Frogman Lager," he said. He reached for a French fry that had fallen onto his chair from somebody's plate, and tossed it to Fred, the resident seagull, who sat in his usual spot, on the railing by the docks.

Fred caught it, and ate it, then watched Reed, to see if he would toss him anything else. He was always on the lookout for more.

"Coming right up," Sheri said, with a sweet smile between her two dimples.

"Shari," Diesel called. "Seen your pilot lately? You could pair up with one of the guys here, and attend my wedding. There will even be swing dancing."

Now that Diesel had found the love of his life, he'd stopped flirting with Sheri, and instead had started trying to fix her up with one of his teammates.

"As much fun as that sounds," she answered with a smile. "We're still together." She picked up an empty glass in front of Rich. "He's flying on an Australia route for one month."

"A month can be a long time," Diesel said. "Just saying."

She shrugged. "He calls me."

She turned to Rich, as she held his glass. "Refill?"

"Just one more," he said. "On my tab this time."

"You've got it." She beamed at him, and then walked away.

The men all watched her go, enjoying the bounce of energy in her step, and the way her hips moved.

"Nice view," Cutter said.

They all agreed.

Even Diesel nodded with a grin.

"On that note, Diesel," Cutter said, "Are you sure you don't want to go see Mermaids, or the Minx Kittens, for your bachelor party?"

"Naw," Diesel said.

A fan of strippers, Cutter knew every stripper in town.

"I can set up a sweet deal, at either club," Cutter said.

I'm good," Diesel said.

He'd settled down after finding Pippa, and their son Bryce. He still enjoyed looking at the waitresses at Chicks, but now he was all about being a good dad to his little boy, and soon, to being a good husband.

"All right, man, but if you change your mind ..." Cutter said, "Just give me the green light, and it's done."

"I'd rather party here, with the team guys who are coming into town for the wedding," Diesel said. "And I can't get too shitfaced. I've got to be ready in time for the wedding, and I need to help Pippa get Bryce ready. Wait till you guys see him." He grinned.

"Yeah, I saw him with Pippa, last week at the commissary," Chris "Fen" Fenner said, grinning back at Diesel. "Little shit kicker looks just like his old man."

Diesel grinned deeper. "Okay, guys," he said. "Now that we're all here ..."

The men quieted to listen to the groom.

"First," Diesel said. "Pippa and I want to thank you, for being in the wedding party. We both really appreciate it."

"No problem, bro," Kik said. "That's what family is for."

SEAL Team XII was indeed a family. A tight one. They watched each other's backs, and looked out for each other's wives, and children.

"Okay, so since Pippa only had immediate family at her first wedding," Diesel leaned back, so Sheri could replace his beer with a new one, then continued. "Because her ex was a controlling ass wipe, she wants the whole nine yards this time," Diesel said. "In her words, a big romantic wedding."

Most of them knew what was coming, as this was not their first rodeo.

"So that means everybody in dress whites' uniforms," he said, "Six swordsmen, and a sword arch," he said.

Several of the men groaned.

Reed knew what they were thinking.

Nobody wanted to put on a uniform, and get a haircut. Even for a wedding. But they would honor the brides wishes, as SEALs always did for their women. Reluctantly, but they would get the groaning over with, before the wedding, and would ensure the bride had that special romantic day she dreamed of.

"We'll even have a small ring bearer," Diesel said. "Pippa ordered a special suit for him."

As he was speaking of Bryce, his three-year-old son by Pippa, who had been rescued by several of the SEALs Team guys, when Pippa and Bryce were taken by her crazy ex, this lightened the general mood considerably.

Everyone on the team had met two-year-old Bryce, that day or shortly afterward, and he had quickly wrapped his little fingers around their hearts.

"How is little man?" Kik asked.

"Excited to be the ring bearer," Diesel grinned. "Pippa has had him practicing, with a cookie on a pillow."

"He doesn't try to eat the cookie?" Daniel "Tractor" Edwards said.

"Only if he drops it, and it breaks," Diesel laughed. "Then he says, 'Oops' and pops half of that cookie into his mouth as fast as he can."

They all laughed.

"Okay, Rich is going to take it from here," Diesel said.

Rich, the Officer in Charge, said, "I need five volunteers. Each swordsman to carry a sword, and form the arch with me."

James "Slim Jim" Slater raised his hand.

Sam Valente, aka "Sammie the conductor, also raised a hand.

Sawyer "Pipes" Ferguson was the third, and "Cutter" Antonius Cutter was the fourth.

Daniel" Tractor" Edwards was the fifth.

"Good," Rich said. "I'll borrow the swords from some other officers. And I want those swords locked up, before the heavy drinking starts. Need I say more."

"No sir," many voices replied.

"On to your hair," Rich said, looking around the room at the men in their dark beards, and long hair. "Either get a haircut, or push your hair under your hat, and use hair gel."

"Yes, sir," they replied.

All of this was in Reed's mind, when Christie asked, "What's the dress code? Are you wearing a tux?"

"White dress uniform," he said.

"Ooh." Her eyes widened. "I've seen those on TV, and I can just imagine you wearing one. "Very formal."

"Yes," he said. "The reception is formal."

"You'll look so handsome in your Navy SEAL white dress uniform. I can't wait to see you in it."

He gave her a tolerant smile, still not thrilled to have to dress up that much.

Give him a wedding on a sandy beach, or in a forest, any day, without all of the frills, and non-essentials.

"Oh, I have the perfect dress," Christie exclaimed with joy.

Excitement filed her, as she thought of the one hanging in the closet.

Silver, with a low halter-style V, and an open back. Like something a movie star would wear.

The special dress she'd never had a place to wear, because her selfish ex would never take her anywhere fancy.

She loved dresses, and dressing up, and weddings. All the fancy things.

"Will there be dancing?" she asked, hoping.

"Yes, ma'am, there will be dancing," he said. "There will even be Swing dancing."

"Oh, good," she said, and gave him a big smile. "I love swing dancing."

Our second date will be perfect. And I can't wait.

~

Two weeks went by fast.

Christie shopped for shoes, to match her dress, and had her hair touched up in the bombshell blonde shade she preferred.

The week of the wedding, Tanya came over to help her do a dress rehearsal, before the big date.

Christie's hair was swept into an up do, with curling tendrils down her back that tickled just a bit.

Tanya put the last finishing touches on the hairdo, and then said, "If he doesn't want to undo this up do, he's not the healthy red-blooded male I think he is. Girl, this tempting hairdo looks like it might tumble down, at any moment, though we know it won't. Maybe he'll want to tumble you, before the evening is over."

"I'm not sure I'm ready to be tumbled," Christie said.

"Reed isn't Mitch," Tanya said. "Girlfriend, he isn't even close to being like Mitch." She moved in front of Christie, and placed her hands on her shoulders. "Reed and you meeting was meant to be. Reed is your fresh start. Don't get cold feet now."

"Cold feet? This is just a date," Christie said. "Not a marriage. Not a moving in together. Not even a 'we're not seeing anyone else'. This is just a date, and it's only our second."

"Just a date?" Tanya pulled back her head and made a face. Then she held her finger up to emphasize what she was saying.

"This is more than just a date. This is him introducing you to all his SEAL buddies; it's also his best friend's wedding. This is where he sees if they approve of you, and if you approve of them. And you know how you get at weddings. Guys know how emotional we get at these events. Girl, this is far more than just a date."

Christie grinned sheepishly. "Okay, so maybe it is more than just a date. But we're still getting to know each other. And it is still only our second date."

"Yes, but *it's a wedding*," Tanya said. "You'll be meeting his friends, and that means he's letting you closer into his inner circle. He may make a move, after the wedding. Lots of guys want to get laid after weddings. And they know we're feeling all emotional, and wanting the romance. Just know what you want, and, if you want him, go for it."

"Okay, okay." Christie put her earrings on. The long dangling earrings she chose, swung when she moved her head.

"Now, those are some sexy earrings," Tanya said. "They're perfect. Go look in the long mirror."

Christie opened the closet door, and looked into the full-length mirror. "Wow."

"Yeah, wow" Tanya said. "And that's just what we want him to think, when you open the door to greet him."

"I think this will do it," Christie said.

"Yeah, I think it will, too." Tanya nodded. "Okay. I'll be here an hour before, to help with your hair and makeup, and then I'll skedaddle, before it's close to time for him to arrive."

"Thanks, Tanya."

"You got it, girl. Now, go shed your glamour, and then let's get a pizza."

"I think I'd better skip pizza this week," Christie said. "The dress is already form-fitting, and if I gain more weight..."

"There will just be more of you to love, and you'll fill out the dress a bit more," Tanya said. "It stretches, you know."

"I know," Christie said. "But it fits perfectly right now."

"Okay, then we'll order a veggie pizza, and drink water," Tanya said. "Because we need to leave enough room for the brownies I made."

"Brownies!"

She loved Tanya's brownies, which were the triple chocolate kind, and bound to add a few pounds to Christies curves.

Tanya grinned. "Yeah, I've been craving chocolate. Needing it bad."

"Why?"

"Oh, girl," Tanya sighed. "You have no idea how bad I need that chocolate. Wait 'til I tell you about Mrs. Vendt."

"Oh no, what's she done now?" Christie turned, and grabbed Tanya's forearm. "Wait. Are Miss Priss, and Brutus all right? She hasn't poisoned them again, I hope."

"No, they're fine," Tanya said. "But she's bought herself a huge water gun, supposedly to rinse off her porch. Then when she sees either of them outside, or doesn't see me, she blasts them with the water gun."

Tanya had planted a border garden between her yard, and Mrs. Vendt's yard, on Tanya's side of the border, and Miss Priss liked to wander through the plants. When she did, Brutus would follow her, sniffing around.

"Are they on your yard, or are they on – "

"On my land of course!" Tanya interrupted, before

Christie could finish. "I try to keep them off her lawn, so they hardly ever go over onto her side anymore, but it doesn't seem to matter. Just seeing them outside makes her mad. Miss Priss has come in soaked three times this week! And Brutus twice."

"So, they're staying on your side, but she's still soaking them anyway, even if though they're not in her yard?"

"Yes!"

"I hate the way she picks on them, as much as you do," Christie said. "I know you worry about them."

Tanya shook her head. "I'm going to have to do something about it. This can't continue."

"Yes, and you can even call the police, and press charges if she breaks the law," Christie said. "If you could catch her on video, being mean to them, then you'd have proof, and she couldn't play innocent. I'll talk to Reed about getting a security system for you. With a video camera. SEALs probably know about things like that."

"Thanks, Christie," Tanya said. "I appreciate it."

"You're welcome," Christie said. "Thanks for helping me get ready for this big date. Hey, go ahead and order that pizza, and I'll get changed. I'll bet your brownies are delicious."

9

———

When Reed knocked On Christie's front door, to pick her up for the wedding, she was in front of her bathroom mirror again, fussing with her hair, double checking that she'd flossed her teeth, and that her makeup looked good. It still felt as if she was forgetting something.

Everything is in place. Must just be my nerves.

"Coming!" she called, as she hurried down the hallway on new silver high heeled shoes which made her taller.

She opened the door, a bit breathless, and still had to look up at Reed, despite the heels. "Hi!" She smiled, taking in how handsome he looked in his white dress uniform, his hair neat, and his face freshly shaken.

He was the most handsome man she had ever seen, and to Christie, looked better than a movie star. Soon they'd be dining and dancing together, and she could not wait.

She kept taking him in with her eyes, hardly able to believe this evening was really happening.

As Christie opened the door, she took Reed's breath away, the way she gave that wide eyed, breathy welcome, and the way she looked, filling out the sexy silver dress.

"Wow," he said. "You are a knockout." He gave her a deep grin. "Hi."

She blushed, charmingly, and dropped her eyelashes, suddenly shy.

The sight of her cleavage, and the way that blush spread across her skin, made him want to uncover the rest of her, to see where else he could make her blush.

But they had a wedding to go to and since it was his best friend's wedding, they couldn't be late.

He would not let R.T. down. Best friends, they always had each other's backs.

"Are you ready?" he asked.

"Oh, yes," she breathed, looking up at him again, her eyes meeting his. "I'm ready."

The moment hovered between them, full of what she might be ready for, before she broke that connection, by saying, "Let me just get my purse."

She turned, and went over to the couch, where a small silver purse sat, and picked it up. Putting the tiny silver chain over her shoulder, she turned back to him and smiled. "All set."

"It's supposed to get cool, later this evening," he said. "You might want to take something." He gestured to the halter dress that left her back and shoulders bare.

"Oh, yes, that's a good idea," she said. Then she opened her closet, and pulled out a silky white shawl.

Reed placed his hand on Christie's lower back, to guide her out the door, and then turned to lock the door behind her.

Soon they were in his car on their way to the wedding.

"What's the bride like?" Christie asked. She looked forward to getting to know his friends. But she knew little about them.

"Pippa is a sweetheart," Cutter said. "And they have a son, Bryce, who is almost three. He'll be the ring bearer."

"Oh!" Christie said. That changed the idea she had in her head about the couple. "That's unusual."

"Everything about how Diesel and Pippa got together is unusual," he said.

"How so?" she asked.

"Diesel and Pippa met at a masquerade party, on Halloween night," Cutter said. "They had a one-night stand, which gave them their son, Bryce. But since they were wearing masks, and didn't exchange names, or phone numbers, they lost contact again, until two years later, when Diesel's dad was visiting, and saw his grandson in the park. He looked just like Diesel, when he was that age. So, he told Diesel, and Diesel started to search for them."

"Oh, wow," Christie said.

"There's more," Cutter said. "Christie had a violent ex-husband, who was in prison. And when Diesel went to see Christie and Bryce for the first time, they'd been taken by her ex."

"Oh no!" Christie said. "How terrible!"

"Diesel called the team," he said. "And we went after them, and got them back. Happy family reunited. Now today, they're making that little family official. Diesel and Pippa will marry, and he's officially adopting his son."

"Oh!" Christie gasped, and placed her hand over her heart, tears glistening in her eyes. "That's real life," Christie said, "But it's also like something out of a movie. What an amazing story."

"It is," he spoke quietly, not unmoved by the little family's story himself. Diesel, Pippa, and Bryce gave him that heart feeling too. "And now they've got another, on the way," he said. "All Diesel can talk about is how he is determined not to miss the birth of this one."

"Oh my goodness," Christie said. "When is she due?"

"She's about three months along," Cutter said. "And Diesel is more excited than I've ever seen him. He missed the birth of his son, but this time he can be part of the whole thing. Unless he's deployed."

"Oh, he could miss the birth?" Christie asked. "I thought the red cross got you guys, and brought you back home, when you had a baby being born."

"Sweetheart where they send us, we may not even be able to tell our own mothers. The Red Cross aren't the ones getting ahold of us," Reed said.

"I see," she said.

"It's not easy being a SEALs wife," he said.

"That would be hard," she agreed. "For both. He'd be missing his child's birth."

"Yes," he said. "It would."

"I hope he can be there, this time," she said.

"I do too," he said.

~

Once inside the church, Christie stood with Reed in the entryway.

She took in the decorations, and especially the floral arrangements. Red roses and white lilies. These weren't flowers she had done. These were done by a competing florist shop.

They were lovely.

"R.T.," another man in uniform said. "Hey man, Diesel is looking for you."

"Be right there," he said. "Christie, this is Osprey." He slid his arm around her back, and looked at Osprey. "This is my girl, Christie." He directed his attention to her again.

"He'll see that you are seated, and if you need anything, let him know. I'll see you after the service," he said.

"Yes, see you then." She smiled at him, as he left to join the wedding party.

After he walked away, she glanced at Osprey.

Tall, dark skinned, with dark hair, and likely native American, his dark brown eyes watched her quietly.

"Nice to meet you," she said. "I don't know anyone else here, yet."

He nodded. "I'll look after you tonight, when R.T. is busy."

"Thank you," she said. "Why do you call him R.T.?"

"Short for railroad tracks," he said.

"That's an interesting nickname," she said.

"A lot of our guys have interesting nicknames," he said. "I'll seat you on the groom's side, since you're with R.T."

"That would be fine," she said.

He held out his arm, and she placed her hand on it, for him to escort her to be seated in one of the pews. Like Reed, his arm was warm, solid muscle.

She realized once she was seated, that many men there were in white Navy dress uniforms.

Everything inside the church, from the stained glass, to the flowers, to the men in uniforms, was visually stunning.

The organist started to play.

Reed, and all the male members of the wedding party ,stood at the front of the church, with the pastor, waiting on the ladies.

One by one, they came down the aisle.

Reed was paired with Pippa's sister, Jeanie Magic Smith, a full breasted woman wearing a dress, which she appeared close to spilling out of.

The dresses were a deep red, which matched the red

roses. The flowers were red roses, and white lilies. Soon everyone was up front, except the ring bearer and the bride.

The moment everyone turned to see three-year-old Bryce, carrying the pillow with the rings on it, Christie got misty eyed.

The little boy, who was the spitting image of his daddy, was adorable in his little suit and tie, as he walked, and looked around at everyone.

He spotted Diesel, halfway down the aisle, and said, "Daddy!" He stopped and waved, then he lifted the pillow up, said, "This is for you, daddy!" then he ran down the aisle toward Diesel.

Everyone laughed.

Diesel took the pillow from his son, and handed it to Reed, who removed the rings, to ready them for the ceremony.

Pippa's mother got little Bryce to sit with her, on her lap, and handed him a cookie.

Then it was the brides turn, to come down the aisle, and the wedding march began to play. When she neared the back of the church, everyone stood, and turned to look at her.

In her long white wedding dress, and lace veil, the bride was stunning.

When the ceremony was over, the bride and groom came down the aisle, and out the front doors of the church.

Everyone stood outside watching them.

Just ahead of the newlywed couple, six SEALs stood, lined up on the steps, three on each side, with swords touching overhead, making a sword arch canopy the newly-weds would walk beneath.

According to the program, Richard "Rich" Irvine, James Slater "Slim Jim", Sam Valente "Sammie the Conductor", Sawyer "Pipes" Ferguson, "Cutter" Antonius Cuttino, and

Daniel "Tractor" Edwards made up the group of men with swords.

"Now may I introduce, Mr. and Mrs. Tanner Taylor," the pastor proclaimed.

Everyone cheered.

The couple began to walk toward the first two SEALs, who lowered their swords to waist level, preventing the couple from passing.

"The first rite of passage is a kiss," Rich said.

A sweet quick kiss followed.

Everyone cheered. The swords were raised again, and the couple moved forward.

But the next two SEALs had now lowered their swords.

Sammie the conductor said, "The price of passage is one kiss."

Diesel kissed Pippa again, and everyone cheered.

The swords were raised again, and the couple took a step forward, but the last two SEALs had lowered their swords, making everyone laugh.

"Laddie, ye must do better than that kiss," Pipes said.

Everyone laughed.

"The price of passage is a real kiss," Pipes continued. "Now sweep her off her feet, man."

Diesel took Pippa into his arms, and dipping her in a romantic swoop, kissed her deeply.

Christie sighed. This was the most romantic wedding she had ever seen.

Diesel and Pippa stood back up, and the final swords were raised.

The couple took a step forward, and Slim Jim lowered his sword to swat Pippa on the butt, making her jump with surprise, and rounded eyes.

Everyone laughed again.

"Welcome to the U.S. Navy, Mrs. Taylor!" he said.

The cheers were even louder now, as every SEAL present raised his voice, to celebrate the newly wedded couple.

Bryce, who'd been released from his grandmother's arms, went racing over to Diesel yelling, "Daddy! Play swords now!"

But the SEALs had immediately returned their swords to their holsters, and all the swords were now safely put away. Soon to be collected by the officer in charge, before the reception got underway.

Diesel picked his son, up as the photographer constantly moved around, taking candid pictures.

Christy couldn't help but smile.

The little boy was adorable, and the new family looked so happy.

Reed and the other SEALs were handsome and fit. She'd never seen so many handsome, fit men, gathered in one place.

Being with him, here, felt like something out of a dream. And the happy little family before her, appeared like every young girl's dream. A strong, handsome, protective husband, an adorable little boy, who that husband clearly loved. A beautiful bride, and a baby on the way.

What a blessing.

It didn't get better than that.

R.T. was by her side now. "Come back inside, while we finish the pictures, and then we'll head over to the reception."

"All right," Christie said, as he placed his hand on her back, to guide her inside.

She quite liked all these good manners, and the way he was protective, and considerate. The way he touched her.

It warmed her inside; in a way she'd never known.

Though Reed had said SEALs did not make the best

husbands, the little girl she had been, could only see the fairy tale perfection of this ceremony today, and the brave, handsome men of SEAL team XII.

Today she found herself disagreeing with him, and believing that one day she might also have that fairy tale.

A perfect husband, a healthy family, and a happy ever after.

It was all she had ever dreamed of.

~

On the way to the reception, Reed watched the road, and the way his date seemed to glow, when talking about the wedding.

"It was the most beautiful wedding I've ever been to," she said, her eyes shining. "Thank you so much for inviting me. I loved the flowers, the dresses, the music, and the ceremony made me cry. But then the sword ceremony," she clasped her hands together. "That was just amazing! Do they do that at every SEAL wedding?"

Reed had not seen Christie so animated before.

She hadn't been kidding, when she'd said she loved weddings.

"Not every wedding," he said. "Only if the bride wants a more formal wedding and requests it."

"You all are so handsome, in your SEAL uniforms," she said. "And your dress whites are elegant."

"Pippa requested we all wear them," he said. "Otherwise, we wouldn't have."

"Oh," Christie said. "Why not?"

"They're uncomfortable as hell," he said. "None of the guys are going to volunteer to wear one." He shrugged. "But for Pippa, not one of us would have let her down. We all got haircuts, and trimmed our beards too."

"Wow," she said. "That's really nice of you."

"We're a family," he said. "That's how we are."

"A Navy family," she said.

"SEAL family," he corrected her. "That's very different. Very tight. The men, and the wives. You'll meet most of them at the reception."

"Your SEAL family," she said with a smile. "I'm looking forward to it. Do you think I will fit in okay?"

10

─────────

"They will love you," Reed said.

He had no doubt of that. Especially the way she looked tonight. He wasn't a jealous man, but this woman was special.

No way was he letting any of the other guys get too close to her tonight. They hadn't been dating that long, and she seemed very caught up in the romance of the military wedding.

She had that dreamy look in her eyes again, as she looked out the window.

He cleared his throat, and she looked at him.

"We're here," he said, as he pulled into the parking lot. After he parked, he gave her a long look.

She quietly watched him back.

"Be sure to save most of your dances for me." He winked at her. "I've been looking forward to that."

And the thought of holding you in my arms.

"I can't wait," she said, joy in her eyes. "Dancing is one of my favorite things to do, especially slow dances."

"I've got things as best man, that must do," he said. "But I will dance with you as much as possible."

"I promise to save all my slow dances for you," she said. "I can wait for you."

Can you, sweetheart? How long can you wait for me when I'm overseas? When you don't even know how long I will be gone?

That 'Dear John' letter he'd received from Becky, though he'd finally burned it one night at a bonfire, while drinking with his SEAL buddies, was burned into his memory. He'd wouldn't think of it now, so he pushed it back.

But it was still behind everything, creating the doubt that would creep in.

"That would be great," he said. "But you don't have to."

He wasn't expecting anything. That way he wouldn't be disappointed in her, or any other woman.

"I want to," she said.

"Ready to go in?"

"Yes," she said, reaching for her shawl, which had slipped down, off one sexy bare shoulder. The way she reached for it, and pulled it back up, as she glanced down, reminded him of how beautiful and how graceful she was.

He got out, and came around to open her door. He scanned the parking lot, helped her out, and then closed the door, and locked it.

Placing his hand on her back again, he guided her into the building, always aware of their surroundings.

With this many SEALs on the property, nothing was going to happen, but the habits were ingrained in him.

Protection was a way of life, situational awareness a constant.

～

T he bride and groom were just inside in a receiving line, with their parents, and their son.

Christie thought the little family was the picture of perfection, as she watched them.

Little Bryce was wanting to shake hands with everyone, just like his daddy. It was clear he looked up to, and adored his dad, who had picked the little fellow up, before he could run about the room, getting into trouble.

"Mr. and Mrs. Taylor, may I present my date, Christie Anderson," Reed said, when they got to the newly married couple.

Diesel took her hand. "Pleased to meet you, Christie," he said with a warm smile. "Glad to see R.T. has a good lady with him, to keep him in line."

With that twinkle in his eyes, Christie wondered what kind of mischief Reed would have gotten into, if she wasn't here with him.

"Thank you," she said. "It's a pleasure meeting you as well."

Moving on to Pippa, Reed said, "You two share an interest in common."

Pippa smiled at them both, waiting to hear what it was.

"You both enjoy dancing, and costumes," Reed said. "Christie likes everything vintage, from the 40's and 50's."

"Then you will have a great time tonight," Pippa told her. "We're going to be swing dancing. It's something I had always wanted to learn. Diesel and I go swing dancing, on date nights."

"Oh, that will be fun," Christie nodded.

It was time for the line to move along, so Reed and Christie moved toward the tables, to look for their names. As he was part of the bridal party, their seats were near the newlywed couple, with a great view of the dance floor.

Soon dinner was served, and Christie was careful not to eat too much. She didn't want anything to interfere with her being able to swing dance.

She wondered, did Reed know how?

Well, she would find out soon enough.

As the dinner plates were being cleared, the music switched to dance music, and Diesel and Pippa took the floor, for their first slow dance as a married couple.

As soon as the floor opened for other dancers, Reed held out his hand to Christie. "Would you like to dance?"

A smile beamed across her face. "Yes, I would love to."

She placed her hand in his, and stood.

He guided her to the dance floor, turned to face her, and pulled her into his arms.

The music, a slow song, suitable for waltzing, was one Christie hadn't heard before, but she liked it.

Later in the evening, after everyone had several cocktails, they all moved to the dance floor, instead of watching the other dancers.

This was totally unlike the last wedding she had been to, where most of the guests preferred watching the others dance, and rarely got up from their seats.

It was clear to Christie that SEALs were doers, and tonight what they were doing was dancing, and celebrating with their SEAL brother, and his new bride.

Little Bryce had fallen asleep, as all the excitement had worn him out, so his grandmother had told the couple good night, and taken him with her, to put him to bed.

Now the couple only had eyes for each other.

It appeared to Christie, that Diesel was wooing his new wife. The romance of this made Christie smile.

Christie was enjoying the dancing.

All twenty SEALs from Reeds team, were on the dance floor having a great time. Matt Hunt, Diesel, Cutter, Rich

Irvine, Osprey, Kik Garcia, Big Mac, Martin Lopez, Chris "Fen" Fenner, Daniel "Tractor" Edwards, Davinci, Tom Campbell, Casper, James "Slim Jim" Ryder, "Pipes" Ferguson, "Sammie the Conductor", "Buzz" Horne, "Numbers" Lewis, Jake Summers.

Reed was dancing with her, and she was enjoying every minute.

Jeanie Magic Smith, Pippa's sister, barely fit into the front of her bridesmaid dress, and was really into the dance.

A ring of men had formed around her, as they all danced and encouraged her, everyone having a good time.

Now that the music had changed, from swing dance to a modern pop tune, Jeanie danced and sang to the tune. As she bounced up and down, singing the lyrics, her breasts bounced.

Nearly all the men's eyes were on her, as if they couldn't look away.

"It's like they're waiting for her to bounce out of that dress," Christie said.

"They are," Reed agreed, and sent her a grin.

Him too?

Christie just shook her head.

Men. They just couldn't help but look.

Changing the subject, she said, "I noticed you hung back from catching the garter."

"I'm in no rush to get married," Reed said. "I'm busy with deployments, or training. Not enough time to give. Most women can't handle that."

Good thing I'm not most women.

Christie kept the thought to herself. For a man like Reed, she wouldn't mind waiting.

"Did you want to catch the bouquet?" he asked.

"No, I would have been embarrassed if I had caught it,"

she said. "I don't really know any of these people. Someone closer to the bride should be the one to catch it."

"Her sister sure wanted it." he said.

"I think her sister likes all the attention of wearing that dress, and bouncing around," she said. "So, she probably liked the thought of the attention she'd get, if she caught the bouquet."

"Maybe so," he said.

The music changed to a slow song she and Reed could dance to, and he swept her into his arms, and across the dance floor.

It was a night she wished would never end.

The next morning, Christie had slept in, and dreamed she was still dancing with Reed.

She woke wishing she could return to the dream.

Padding into the kitchen on bare feet, Christie started her coffee, and then got out eggs to cook, and bread to toast. She'd just finished scrambling the eggs, and her toast had popped, when her phone rang.

She saw it was Tanya, and answered. "Hello?"

"Hey girl, are you alone?"

"Yes," she answered slowly, wondering why Tanya was asking.

Christie was still getting to know Reed. It had only been their second date, and she had to make sure he wasn't a heavy drinker, before she could get serious with him.

"I've got an errand to run, out your way, and thought I'd stop by after," Tanya said. "But I wanted to be sure you weren't still entertaining your man."

"Nope, not entertaining," Christie said. "Just home,

relaxing. I'd love it if you stopped by. Have you had breakfast?"

"Heck yeah," Tanya said. "Had my usual bagel, and then walked the dogs. I'll be around in about an hour."

"Sounds good," Christine said. "See you then."

"Great! I want to hear all about your date with Reed! See you soon."

Christie hung up, and her thoughts returned to Reed.

Would he turn out to be her long-term boyfriend?

He doesn't seem to be dating anyone else.

The first time they'd gone out, he'd asked her out again, before the first date was even over. This time, on their second date, he hadn't asked her out again; he'd just brought her home.

Should I have invited him in?

The date had been wonderful. The dancing, the beautiful setting, that kiss he'd left her with.

She'd hoped he would ask her out again. Maybe he would, soon.

If he wanted to be her long-term boyfriend, she was ready.

Long term though, that meant sex. And he's so fit. Super fit. Muscular with very little fat.

She glanced down at her curves.

Whereas I'm all curves, and not very muscular. I'm not exactly the super fit, hang out at the gym, kind of woman.

Prior to meeting Reed, that hadn't been a concern.

She was happy with herself, and her life. She didn't look in the mirror and see one hundred things wrong with her, the way she had done when she was younger.

She saw curves, and her bright shining eyes, and her smile. She hoped that was what Reed saw when he looked at her.

Maybe he did. He'd asked her out twice, in a short

period of time. He'd been making an effort to get to know her. Which meant he must be interested in things going further.

She wanted that too.

Why does that thought make me so nervous?

11

Christie stood at her closet, eyeing the red and white checked dress that she'd worn to the movie premiere. She'd worn it for only a few hours, and later despaired that the blood stains might have ruined it.

She'd worked hard on the dress, soaking it, and then scrubbing it, to get the stains out. It wasn't as white as it had been, but she'd taken a brush, and painted bleach on it, and then had rinsed it out again, until the stains weren't noticeable.

Maybe I could wear the dress again.

Her phone rang.

Reed.

She answered it. "Hello?"

"Hello," she said. "How are things?"

"Busy," he said. "I wanted to check on you, and see how you are doing."

"Good," she said. "It's really nice to hear from you."

"I'd like to take you to dinner," he said. "Saturday night, if you're free."

"Yes, I'd love to have dinner with you, Saturday," she said.

"Great," he said. "I'll make reservations, and surprise you."

A thrill shivered through her. "Oh, I like surprises."

"That's good," he said. "Now, I have a request."

"You do?" She hoped it was something she could accommodate. "Okay, what is your request?"

"That red and white checked dress you wore, the night we met. Was it ruined? Can you still wear it?"

Her eyes widened. It was as if he'd been reading her mind. Now he *wanted* her to wear the vintage dress.

"Yes, I can wear it," she said. "I'd be happy to wear it. I didn't know you liked it."

"Yeah, I liked it." His husky voice sent a feeling through her that warmed her inside.

"Oh, I'm so glad," she said, her voice lower now, and breathy.

"You looked hot in that dress," he said.

He'd said hot. He must be thinking of sex. So, he is interested in me that way.

"Thank you," she said.

"Wearing a dress like that," he said. "Someone should be taking you out to a nice dinner."

"That would be lovely," she said.

"Great," he said. "I'll pick you up at seven Saturday."

"Perfect," she said. "I'll be ready."

R eed watched Christie moving in the red and white dress.

She was like visual candy.

Thoughts of her in that dress, and then her stepping out of that dress, had become his new favorite fantasy.

They were seated, and then the waiter took their drink order.

He returned with a bottle of red wine, and then offered Reed a taste.

Reed took a sip, and okayed it.

The waiter poured them each a glass, took their orders, and then left.

Christie took a sip of her wine, and began to speak. "It's nice to relax," she said. "I haven't really done that, since the shooting. Being around you relaxes me. And I haven't ever had lobster ravioli before."

"I'm sorry to hear you're not sleeping," he said. "But glad you can relax with me. I think you'll like the ravioli, but if you don't, I'll share half of my lasagna. The portion sizes here are generous."

She took another sip, and smiled at him. "Thank you." She set her glass down, and put her hand in her lap, to smooth out her napkin, and her nerves.

Christie looked up at him again, and brought up the first topic she'd wanted to talk to him about.

"I'm thinking about getting a dog. Well, a puppy really. Because I live alone. I think I'll feel safer with a dog. I've been wanting to get a puppy for a while, anyway."

"A dog would be good." He nodded. "What kind?"

"A German Shepherd," she said.

"Good choice," he said.

"My friend Tanya has one. He's the one her neighbor, Mrs. Vendt, tried to poison, along with her cat."

"You're sure the neighbor poisoned them?"

"Well, we don't have proof, but I'm sure it was her." Christie frowned. "She hates them."

"Hmm," he said. He watched, as the waiter brought them bread to munch on, before speaking again.

Once the waiter left, he said, "Has your friend told the police?"

"No, because we have no proof," Christie said.

"That's one thing police do," he said. "Look for proof. They have the training that you and Tanya don't have."

When she continued to frown, he changed the subject.

"Have you thought about getting a handgun?" he asked.

"Yes, I have," she said. "I ought to buy a gun for my protection at home. But I've no idea what to get. I don't feel comfortable with the big guns. I'd get a small handgun, but that won't do any good against a man with a big automatic gun, like the theater shooter. I wouldn't know what to do against someone like him."

Reed watched, and listened, waiting until she'd finished speaking. "Let's talk about that. Why do you think the shooter wasn't able to do more damage?"

"Because you stopped him," she said.

"That's part of the reason," he said. "He had the bigger gun. I had the handgun. Why did I win?"

"Because you're a Navy SEAL."

He liked the way she said that, so instinctively, because it made him feel like Superman. "One thing SEALs do constantly, is train. I know my guns like I know my own hand."

"You won with a handgun, a smaller gun, because you were trained," she said.

"Right. Training is key to winning." Reed nodded. "The other thing is, these idiots who want to shoot up a theater, or any other public place full of civilians, think fully automatic will cause more damage, so they don't bother aiming, and they end up causing less damage than if they'd used a pistol more carefully. Big gun doesn't always mean big win."

She frowned. "But they have more bullets."

"Having more bullets, and rapid fire, does not mean

accuracy." He tilted his head. "You like vintage things. Think back to the 1920s. You've seen movies with the tommy guns, right? Thompson submachine guns?"

"Yes," she nodded. "I have. I love the 1920s dresses, but those guns are scary."

"Those are some of the most inaccurate guns ever made," he said. "They were heavy, and pulled up when you shot them. The shots would spray." He moved his arm in an arc, up and over. "Like this."

She watched as he demonstrated.

"So, if you're aiming at a guy, you might hit him," he said. "But if you didn't hit him at first, already the gun would be moving, and you'd be fighting to control its aim. It's not an easy gun to shoot. Modern guns are more accurate, but the same principals apply."

"So, I'd need to go to the range and train," she said.

"Absolutely," he said. "I'd be happy to train you."

"Okay, so maybe I can try some of the other handguns, and find one that is easier to use." She glanced down at her small hands. "I might need one of those tiny guns, like women used to hide in their dresses."

His large, warm hand closed over hers. "We'll find you one that fits your hand, but isn't too small to be effective."

"Okay." She smiled.

"Would you like to go to the range next week?" He asked. "Tuesday night I'm free."

"Yes," she said. "I would like that."

He continued to hold her hand, and then gave it a squeeze, before letting go, as the waiter placed their plates in front of them.

Their Italian food all looked delicious, the music was restful, and the restaurant was dark, and romantic.

To Christie, it was a perfect date.

And when he brought her home, walked her to the front

door, and bent down to kiss her, she wanted to freeze the moment in her memory forever.

That kiss. It was everything she'd ever dreamed of.

He gently claimed her lips, as if he was the only one meant to kiss them, as if he treasured her, but underlying that was an intensity he held back.

It was a wooing kiss, and she wanted more. Oh, so much more.

She wrapped her arms around his neck, and pulled him closer.

His tongue slipped between her lips, to meet her tongue, and their tongues touched, tentative, and then, dancing together, moved faster. The intensity ramped up, until they broke apart each needing air.

"Wow," she said.

He was thinking the same thing. He'd kissed a lot of women.

But none of them were Christie.

Sweet, sexy, delicious, Christy.

He could have kissed her all night.

She seemed a little dazed, and maybe that was the wine. She took a step, and wobbled a little on her heels.

He reached out to hold her, keeping her from falling.

"Oops," she said. "Maybe I'm a little tipsy. Either that, or you made me dizzy."

He looked at her closely. "Tipsy, probably," he said.

"I'll be okay, once I sit down," she said.

He helped her unlock her door, and then guided her inside.

She sat down on the closest chair. Not the couch, he noted. He couldn't tell if she wanted him to stay, or if she was ready for him to leave.

"Thank you for taking me to dinner," she said. "And to the wedding, and to the range to learn to shoot."

"My pleasure," he said. "So, next Tuesday I'll take you shooting again."

"Yes," she nodded, then leaned back against the chair, and closed her eyes.

That was his cue.

She must be sleepy. Maybe she'll sleep well tonight.

"All right, sweetheart, I'll let myself out, and lock up for you. Good night."

"Night," she murmured.

He bent to kiss the top of her head, and then turned to let himself out.

Early on Tuesday morning, before the sun was even close to rising, Christie woke, groggy, and with a feeling something was wrong.

She heard a strange noise in the other room, which must have awakened her.

She had to lie very still and silent, listening.

Someone is moving in the other room.

Who is in my house? The burglar on the news, who'd been breaking into houses? It had happened in a different neighborhood, and those people weren't at home.

Oh my God, I bet it's him. What will he do, if he knows I'm home? What if he has a knife, or a gun?

She reached for her cellphone, and dialed Reed.

He didn't pick up, but his answering message did.

She whispered into the phone, "Reed, someone is in my house. In the other room. I don't know what to do."

The sounds were getting nearer.

She pulled the phone under the covers, and placed it face down, so the light wouldn't show. Turning the phone to mute, it would now be silent, and Reed would be able to hear.

The door to her room started to open.

Frozen in her bed, Christie closed her eyes, and stilled her breathing, trying to appear asleep, and waited for what would happen next.

Her heart raced.

Maybe he'll think I'm asleep. Please God.

The door to her room started to open.

12

———

Not daring to peek, even a little, Christie stayed as still as she could, hoping that the thumping of her heart didn't give away the fact she was awake.

The intruder moved to her dresser and opened a drawer. The telltale sound of the drawer scraping, as he pulled it open, told her what was going on.

She tried to control her breathing; sure that he could hear her.

Rummaging in the drawer, he then moved on to the next one, doing the same. Other sounds came then.

Maybe he's taking something.

Suddenly the sounds stopped.

She heard nothing but silence, and her own breathing.

Oh my God. Where is he?

Her heart thumped doubly loud in her chest, and she prayed he didn't hear it, and guess she was awake.

Then she heard him breathing.

He was standing at the foot of her bed, breathing. Not moving.

Oh my God. He's looking at me. Watching me.

She felt it. Sensed it. Pinpricks of fear spread across her body, raising goose bumps.

Would he see them?

Or see her breathing, and know she wasn't asleep?

He stood watching and listening, for what felt like forever. And then he moved toward the door.

Still praying, she waited. And waited. Until her bladder felt like it would burst.

Is he gone?

The house was silent. No one was in the bedroom.

He hadn't closed the door all the way, and she peeked at the door.

A crack showed the hallway. She eyed that crack, and then dared to glance at her phone.

Thirty minutes had gone by.

No response from Reed. He must not have received her message.

Slowly she crept out of bed, into her bathroom, and closed and locked the door.

Then she dialed 911.

How did he get in?

She needed to find out, but she didn't want to leave the safety of the bathroom, until the police got there.

Dialing 911, she was determined to wait until the police arrived, before coming out.

She just hoped the burglar wasn't still in the house.

The wait seemed to take forever.

When the police arrived, with lights and siren, she came out of the bathroom, to answer the front door, after grabbing her robe to wrap around her pajamas.

It felt safe to go back into her bedroom to get it, because the bad guy wouldn't stick around if the police were there.

The lights would've scared him off.

She let the officers in, after they both held up their

badges for her to read, and then a kind officer named Tom O'Malley took her initial statement, while Officer Skip Teagan looked around for any evidence.

Officer Teagan found an open window, in the living room on the side wall, with the lock, and the glass broken.

"This is where he gained entry," Officer Teagan said.

"He could have hidden behind those bushes, and no one would have seen him breaking the window from the road," Officer Tom O'Malley said, then he turned back to Christie. "You might want to have that tall, wide bush on the corner trimmed, Miss."

"Please call me Christie," she said. "I don't know how I slept through that window breaking! I don't like to think what he might have done to me if he'd known I was awake!"

"From the pattern of the break, and the glass, it may not have made much noise," the officer said. "It looks like a professional broke in. The same pattern you've likely heard about, on the news. Don't beat yourself up over this, Christie. You did the right thing, playing possum." He gave her an encouraging smile.

"My boss told me about the break-ins," she said. "I haven't been watching the news, since the live shooting in the theatre."

"Where you there?" Officer O'Malley asked.

"Yes," she nodded. "I helped put the tourniquet on that other man."

"That was a fine thing you did, Christie." He nodded, smiling at her.

She blushed red, and shifted on the couch, uncomfortable by the attention.

"Well, Miss Christie, can you look around, and see if anything is missing? If so, we'll need a list from you."

"Oh, yes, of course," she said. "Oh, and I haven't even

offered you both anything to drink yet. Where are my manners? I can make coffee."

"Your manners are just fine, and we thank you for the offer, but we don't need any coffee." He waved the coffee off with his hand. "Just concentrate right now, on seeing if anything has been taken."

She went into her bedroom, and opened the top drawer in her dresser, where she usually stored her jewelry.

"All my jewelry is gone," she said looking up at Officer O'Malley.

The jewelry box was empty.

It appeared the thief had grabbed everything in it, her costume jewelry, and the good jewelry she'd inherited from her grandmother. Tears filled her eyes.

Everything from grandmother is gone.

"I need you to try to remember everything that was in your jewelry box," Officer O'Malley said. "Jewelry, money, keys."

"Keys?" she asked.

He nodded. "Many women store keys with their jewelry. Car keys, house keys, keys to safety deposit boxes."

"Oh." She wrinkled her forehead. "No, I never put keys in there. But grandmothers' jewelry was. I'd better list that. Some of mine was costume though. I doubt he could resell any of that."

"List everything that's been taken," Officer O'Malley said. "The insurance company will sort the values out. And a good description will help us, if it turns up at a local pawn shop."

She started a list of everything she could remember being in the drawer.

Once the police were done taking her statement, and had written down everything, they were ready to go.

Officer O'Malley stood. "Christie, I hope if you're ever in

a situation again, that you'll call 911 first, not your SEAL friend. Even Mr. Tindall called 911. Our dispatchers are always on the job, twenty-four seven, and will stay on the line with you."

"Oh, yes, I see what you mean," she said. "In the theater he stopped the man, and then called 911. They stayed on the line, talking to me, until I had to help him put a tourniquet on the other man. I guess I should've thought of calling you first, when the thief broke in."

"Hopefully you won't have any more problems, but here's my card if you do, or if you have questions about the robbery." He handed her his card. "And if any of your jewelry turns up, we'll let you know."

The card had Officer O'Malley's number on it.

"Thank you," she said. "I really appreciate that."

Once they'd left, she locked the door behind them, and then went back to bed and tried to sleep.

It was impossible to relax enough to sleep.

Finally, she got up, and fixed herself a bowl of cereal, then fired up her computer.

By morning, when the sun rose, she'd already looked up places that could come out and repair the glass, and she started calling them as soon as they opened.

The sooner she could get the window repaired the better.

After she'd found a man who could come out that day to fix it, she hung up, and called her best friend.

"Hey, you're up early," Tanya said.

"Yes. Well, I haven't slept. I may never sleep in my own bed again," Christie said.

"Oh no. Why not?"

"A burglar broke in last night, and stole all my jewelry, while I was in bed asleep."

"Oh, my God," Tanya said. "You're kidding."

"Not kidding. I stayed in bed, not moving, while he robbed me, and then waited until he left, and called the police."

"Oh, girl, you must've been terrified."

"I was," Christie said. "Literally could not move. Frozen like an ice sculpture, under the covers. And the creepiest, scariest part? He stopped at the foot of my bed, and stood there, and watched me."

Tanya gasped.

"I didn't know what he would do!" she said. "It was terrifying! He watched, probably to make sure I was asleep, and then he left."

"Thank God for that," Tanya said. "I'm so glad you're okay."

"Me, too," Christie said.

"Oh my God, girlfriend!" Tanya said, "You have the worst luck, with crazy stuff happening, and the best luck, at coming through without getting hurt."

"Right?!" Christie said.

"I'm coming over," Tanya said. "No arguing with me. It's what I should've done the last time. I'll bring chocolate covered donuts, and a great big hug. You make the coffee."

"Okay. That sounds good." Christie wasn't going to argue with Tanya. This time she knew she really needed that hug.

13

───────

Wednesday, the window was repaired, and Tanya spent the whole day with her, after Christie called into work, and explained the situation.

Christie stayed in her pajamas, wrapped in her grandmother's quilt, on the couch. and watched old movies. She didn't feel like going anywhere, but also no longer felt safe in her own home.

Her phone rang, but it wasn't Reed.

By Wednesday night, Reed still hadn't called her back. Something she was trying not to think about, because she didn't understand why he'd gone silent.

Especially given the message she'd left on his phone Tuesday night.

Tanya called Thursday morning.

Christie answered. "Hello?"

"If you still want a German Shepard puppy, you'd better move fast. I just called the breeders this morning, to ask about puppies for you. They have four eight-week-old puppies, and one has already been sold. They sell fast. So, we need to go today. Are you ready?"

"Yes," Christie said.

If she'd had a puppy, to bark at the intruder, he might not have entered her house. He wouldn't have been able to stand at the bottom of her bed, watching her.

"Good. I'll call them back, and tell them we'll be there in an hour. Throw your shoes on, and be ready to go," Tanya said.

"Okay." Christie thought about her plans for the day, and mentally went down her list.

There was nothing that couldn't be rescheduled. This was important.

"Bye."

"Bye." Christie hung up the phone, and started looking for her shoes, as excitement started to run through her.

I'm going to get a puppy! This is better than Christmas.

Even if the recent scare was now part of her motivation. She was getting a puppy!

She found her shoes, her purse, and her car keys. Though it sounded like Tanya was driving.

Christie could hardly wait. She loved animals, dogs especially, and now she'd have one of her own. A German Shepherd like Tanya's sweet dog, Brutus.

Two hours later, they were home with eight-week-old Lacey. Tanya had put one of her dog crates in the back seat of her car, and the puppy had ridden in it.

They'd stopped at the pet store, to get food and water bowls, a new collar and leash, doggie shampoo, treats, and several toys. The pet store was one where you could take your dog inside with you.

Lacey wagged her tail at everyone, and sniffed nearly everything in the store.

Her excitement was contagious.

Now at home, the puppy was free to sniff everything in the house, and the tail wagging, and sniffing commenced.

Tanya went into the kitchen, and came back out with

paper towels, and cleaning spray. "She's going to pee all over the place, until you get her trained, and she settles down. With all this excitement, she's going to have accidents."

"Oh, I know puppies do that." Christie nodded. "We had a couple of dogs, when I was growing up, and got them both as puppies. I remember. I also remember they don't sleep much at night, at first."

"No, they don't," Tanya agreed. "I hope you're prepared for all that."

"It can't be any worse than when the burglar broke in," Christie said. "That was nearly as terrifying as the shooting at the theater. Honestly, I haven't been sleeping well since that happened."

"I'll bet," Tanya said. "I'm so glad you decided to get Lacey. She'll bark, and scare any burglars away."

"Yes, she will." Christie smiled. "And she'll be my constant companion. Except when I'm at work."

"Remember what I said about crating her. If you let her have the run of the house, she'll chew up things while you're gone. Puppies love to chew."

"Yes, I will. Do you think I should look for a pet sitter, or a doggie day care? She'll be home by herself, when I'm at work."

"Can you come home for lunch, to let her out?" Tanya asked.

"I'm pretty sure Mrs. Brown will let me go a few minutes over, if I explain what I'm doing," Christie said. "I often stay late, when we have big orders, and she knows the work will get done."

"Okay, good," Tanya nodded. "Then I don't think you need a dog sitter."

They played with Lacey for a while, and then Tanya left.

Christie couldn't wait to get settled into her new routine, just her and Lacey.

She still hadn't heard from Reed, but now she had a new puppy to keep her busy.

Who needs a man, anyway? The two of us will be just fine.

~

He needed to call Christie, and explain he'd been called away on a mission, and he needed to ask if she was willing to reschedule their date.

The minute he was able to use his cell phone again, Reed pushed the button, to listen to voice messages, and then frowned.

His frown grew deeper the longer he listened.

Immediately, he dialed Christie's number.

No answer.

"Christie, are you all right? I just got your message. Damn, I hope you're okay. Call me."

He hung up the phone, and scowled. It had been four days since she'd called, terrified that someone had broken into her house. First was the message, then the long pause, and finally the breathing, and the hang up. Anything could've happened.

It was Saturday, and he'd received no other calls since the first one.

This is not good.

He had to find her, as soon as he left the base.

If she wasn't home, he'd try the florist shop.

~

It was dark when he pulled up to her house, and saw her lights on.

She's at home. Why hasn't she called me back?

He got out, walked to the front door, and knocked.

Inside, a dog started to bark.

She opened the door with a German Shepard pup at her feet, who stood furiously barking at Reed.

She was safe.

Relief flooded through him.

She appeared safe. But pale.

"Come in," she said, without smiling, her voice brittle, unspoken anger in her tone. "Meet Lacey."

His stomach tightened. This wasn't the greeting he'd expected. So few words. Not even the trace of a smile. And she was angry.

They hadn't seen each other in over a week.

Is she even glad I'm back? Things were fine when I left.

Frustration coursed through him.

Damn it.

He had to fix this.

"Hello, Lacey," he said then he looked at Christy. "Can I come in?"

She picked up the puppy, and stepped back, to let him in, but she still didn't speak.

The puppy barked at him as he stepped inside.

"Nice dog," he said. "When did you get her?"

"After the break-in," she said with a shrug.

"So, you did have an intruder. Damn."

He closed his eyes, for only a second. When he looked at her again, he noted she was watching his face.

She was so reserved, tonight. Not the smiling, happy woman he knew. She was upset.

Upset enough to get a German Shepard puppy.

Has she moved on? Can she see my regret?

"I got your phone message, only an hour ago," he said. "I couldn't use my phone before then."

"Yeah, I heard your message, when I got home from the pet store," she said.

He shook his head. "Why didn't you call me back?"

She shrugged.

He raked a hand through his hair. "I was worried."

Her tone brittle, she said, "Well, you're a little late to be worried. The break-in was days ago."

His shoulders fell. "I was deployed."

"And you couldn't say, 'Hey Christie, I'll be away'? Don't wait for me Tuesday night. I can't go to the range?"

"No, this time I couldn't," he said.

He had to make her understand.

"Sometimes . . . we can't. The order comes, and there's no time. We must leave right away."

He wanted to reach for her, to hold her, but this was important. They needed to straighten this out. He wanted to work things out between them, but if she couldn't accept this part of his life, there wasn't any point trying. Because it would never work long term. And the headspace she was in right now, would be stuck on repeat.

"That's a Navy SEAL's life, Christie," he said, his voice roughening. "Not every woman can handle that. It's especially hard on wives, and children."

She was silent for a moment, her narrowed gaze still studying his face.

But then she squared her shoulders. "I can handle it. I have a dog now, and I'm going to get a gun. I don't need a man to protect me."

Is she saying she doesn't need me? Doesn't want me around? Is it over between us?

What we have is good. Worth fighting for. If she'll fight for us, with me.

He watched her, assessing.

The defiant way she'd spoken, made him wonder.

She wasn't the fighting type, and she'd had no training, just one visit to a gun range.

He noted the way her jaw, jutted just a little, as she stood there, holding her dog.

Despite what she'd said, it didn't look like she was handling being a SEAL's girlfriend very well. She had that 'my feelings are hurt' look some women got.

"Tell me about the break in," he said, wanting to know, and wanting to straighten things out between them. "You sounded terrified, being in the house with an intruder."

She put the dog down.

Lacey started sniffing his feet, but she had stopped barking at him.

They both watched her for a moment.

"I was terrified," Christie finally admitted, opening to him to share her story. "I stayed very still, under the covers, and hoped he didn't know I was awake."

Froze, he thought. *What she did was freeze.*

He'd seen how she reacted to danger.

Hunker down, and hands over her head, was her go to reaction.

He would bet she'd had those covers over her head, shaking.

That was not good.

But he could train the freeze out of her . . .

"So, you stayed real still," he said. "Then what happened?"

"He stopped at the foot of my bed, and watched me."

He sucked in a breath. Fought the surge of anger that rose swiftly inside of him.

He'd been holding it back, trying to listen.

It was always harder to listen, when you got angry.

"How do you know it was a man? Did you get a good look at him?"

"No, but most burglars are men," she said.

"Don't be so sure," he said. "It could've been a woman."

She crossed her arms. "Well, this burglar, whatever he, or she was, stared at me."

Damn. She had to have been terrified.

"Then what happened?"

"He left. With all my jewelry. Most of it was costume, but he got a few nice pieces, that were my grandmothers, that could bring money."

"That really sucks, and I hate that it happened to you. But I'm glad you weren't hurt."

"He got in through a window, but I had it replaced. And I got Lacey."

"Good. Sounds like you handled things well, and she's a great pup." He held out his hand to Lacey.

Lacey, done with sniffing Reed's shoes, and barking at him, came near to sniff the hand he held down for her.

When she started licking his hand, Christie uncrossed her arms, and chuckled softly. "She likes you."

"Dogs always do."

Christie smiled, some of her hurt feelings over his desertion soothed, now that she understood the cause.

He seemed genuinely regretful over the fact he hadn't been able to warn her.

Reed hadn't been playing mind games, he really had a job which didn't allow him to tell people where he was going, and what he was doing, or when he would be back.

She believed him, and trusted him. With her life. And he'd been nothing but honorable since she'd met him.

Reed sat on the couch, playing with the puppy while she watched.

If she'd thought he was handsome before, watching him play with the puppy made him even more attractive.

Then it hit her.

I am head over heels in love with this man. Everything about him.

"I'm glad you have a guard dog now," he said. "You'll need to train her."

"I plan to," she said. "I already signed up for obedience lessons on Saturdays. Mrs. Brown was nice enough to agree to give me Saturdays off, starting next week. For several weeks in a row, which is a lot in the florist business. But she agrees I need to train Lacey. So, I'll be working late, on some Friday nights when she needs me."

"How late?"

"However long it takes to get the arrangements done."

"Sweetheart, it's time to get serious about getting the handgun you were thinking about. Since you can't take your new guard dog everywhere you go. And since I'm often called away, out of the country, I'd feel better, knowing you were taking measures for your safety."

Oh, he's worried about my safety. He must care for me.

The thought made her feel warm inside.

"I was scared when the guy broke into my house," she said. "I froze. What if I do that when I have a gun? The bad guy might take it from me, and then I'd be even worse off."

"That's true, you would," he said. "This is why we train. So, we don't freeze, and instead, go into the moves we've practiced. I can train you past the freeze point--if you're willing."

"I'm willing," she nodded.

"Good. Now let's talk about getting you set up with a security system. I could install it for you."

"Oh, that's a great idea. Thank you. My friend Tanya needs one too. Because of her crazy neighbor, Mrs. Vendt, who hates Tanya's cat and dog."

"I could put one in for her," he said. "After I set yours up."

"That would be great," she said.

"Turn on your laptop," he said. "And we'll look at some different set ups for security."

They spent the rest of the evening looking at things she could do to be more secure, and they talked late into the night.

It was good to have him back in her life, and to know he'd never really left her. But he had been deployed. And that made a big difference.

He was right, it would be hard when he deployed, but she had Lacey now, for protection and companionship, and he was focused on making sure she would be safe, when he wasn't around to protect her.

When he was with her, she was very happy, and he was present and attentive with her.

Before he left that night, they had a plan for her security. He would put up camera's, he would take her shopping for a handgun, and would continue to train her on it. And she had Lacey, who had been very protective at first, when he had arrived.

At the door, before they said goodbye, he said, "I've missed you. The whole time I was gone."

"I missed you too," she said. "I'm glad you're back."

He dipped her into one of those sweeping kisses, like Diesel had swept Pippa at their wedding.

Oh my. He really did miss me, she thought.

Then she forgot everything else but the kissing.

After two months of dog training, firearms training, and self-defense training, the woman Reed picked up for their Tuesday night date at the range looked the same, and yet different.

Christie still walked out the door in one of those sexy

retro outfits, after punching in the code on the new alarm on her house, but instead of stepping tentatively on those high heels, she strode.

She strode in, wearing her new boots, like a woman who had confidence, who would look a man in the eye, instead of blushing and looking down. She was a perfect mix of feminine and aware.

Not the first female a predator would target.

And that gave Reed great satisfaction.

She didn't have a victim's mindset.

After what had happened in the theater, and then the break in at her house, she could so easily have gone the other way.

He was glad she hadn't, and he was prouder of her than he could say.

She stepped into his car, and he waited until she was settled, before closing her door.

He could envision doing this for the rest of their lives, and soon, he would tell her so, and see what her thoughts were on that.

Driving to the restaurant for dinner, he asked, "Did the police ever find your jewelry, at any of the pawn shops?"

"No, they didn't recover a thing." Christie shook her head. "It's just gone."

"That's a shame," he said. "Have you thought about replacing things?"

"Yes, but I just haven't yet," she said. "I probably look plain, without any jewelry."

She did look plainer, when he was used to her wearing her sparkling things, but she looked beautiful to him, without all of that. And he would make sure to tell her so.

"You look beautiful," he said.

"I just feel so bare, without my jewelry," she said.

"Open the glovebox," he said, looking forward to seeing her reaction.

She gave him a puzzled look, but then she reached for it. Opening the glovebox, she looked inside.

A small box sat inside.

"Open it," he said.

She pulled the box out, and lifted the lid.

Inside were gold hoop earrings.

"Oh, wow! I love them!" she said, her eyes sparking.

"I had to ask the jewelry clerk for help," he said. "I told them retro style, or vintage. I'm not up on all that. I told her you liked 40's and 50's style. Then she showed me a whole line of 1950's jewelry."

"You did great!" Christine said, "This is the style Marilyn Monroe wore! I could show you pictures."

He grinned. "I'm glad you like them."

"Like them? I love them," she said.

She was already putting them on.

"Wait till I tell Tanya!"

"I thought you could wear them to the cookout next weekend," he said.

"There's a cookout?"

"Yes. Now that Diesel and Pippa are back from their honeymoon and his deployment, they want to throw a big party. He's got a new grill to try out."

"Oh, that will be fun. I didn't really get to talk to her much, at the wedding, but she seemed nice."

"She is," he nodded. "You can invite Tanya if you'd like."

Tanya kept telling Christie that she wished she could meet a hot Navy SEAL, and Christie had finally mentioned it to Reed.

"Oh thanks, she would love that," Christie said. "Wait till I tell her. Is it next Saturday?"

"Sure is," he said.

"Perfect."

Christie moved her head from side to side, looking at

her new earrings in the mirror over the dash. "These earrings are perfect too."

"I'm glad you like them," he said. "They look great on you. It's good to see you looking so happy."

She beamed at him, and he smiled back.

"I wish every day would be a perfect day like this one," she said. "I love it when we have a day together."

He would be away from the base, training soon.

SEALs were always training, somewhere.

"I like spending my days with you, too," he said.

He was almost ready to talk to her about their future, but still he held back. That old dear John letter had done a number on his head. He knew it, but hadn't quite kicked it to the curb, yet.

Another week or two couldn't hurt, if he wasn't deployed before they talked about it.

"Picnics are one of my favorite things," she said, still beaming.

Learning her favorite things gave him satisfaction, because then he knew how to surprise her, and bring that sunny smile more often, which was rapidly becoming one of his favorite things to do.

~

Tanya rode with them to the barbecue and was attending as their guest.

Reed introduced her to Diesel and Pippa, their hosts, and then to a few of the guys.

It was clear she loved meeting all these SEALs, but she appeared thunderstruck now, and she stood looking past he and Christie.

Someone had arrived, and she was frozen to the spot.

Reed turned and saw "Casper" standing near the gate to the back yard. He should have known.

The man had a way of entering a room, and leaving it, without anyone knowing he was there. It was a rare and valuable skill set, which saved lives. He should have been in the CIA, but maybe he had been, or maybe he still was.

Christie turned to look too, after seeing the reaction of her best friend. "Oh, that's Casper," she said to her.

"Casper," Tanya whispered. "Is that his real name?"

"No, that's his nickname," Reed said. "Given because he can enter a room without you knowing he is there."

"How cool," Tanya said, clearly in hero worship mode.

"His real name is Scott Roberts," he said. "Come on, I'll introduce him to you."

Eyes wide, Tanya just nodded, then she walked with him to where Scott stood.

Christie stayed where she was, watching them.

I've never seen her like this. Tanya must have it bad for Casper.

The last thing she needs is another female nearby, when they meet for the first time.

It appeared that Casper was as delighted to meet Tanya, as she was to meet him.

Soon Reed was back by her side. "Those two hit it off well," he said.

"I could tell that from way over here," Christie said. "Is he a good guy?"

Reed gave her a look. "I wouldn't introduce her to one who isn't," he said.

"Good, because I don't want her to get her heart broken."

"I wouldn't want him to, either." Reed gestured to the tables full of food. "Ready to fill a plate?"

"Yes, more than ready," she said.

They enjoyed burgers and brats on buns, potato salad,

coleslaw, baked beans, corn on the cob, and sliced wedges of watermelon for dessert.

When they finished, Reed said, "Want to go for a stroll?"

"Yes, of course," she said.

He gave a signal to Diesel, and they headed for the gate.

"What did you tell him?" Christie asked.

"That we'd be back shortly," he said.

"It's fascinating the way you guys can talk to each other without speaking," she said. "Do you use that all the time?"

"When it's needed," he said.

She smiled at him, and he threaded his fingers through hers. "Have I told you how pretty you look tonight?"

She shook her head no.

"Well, you do." He made a note to himself to tell her that more often. He wasn't used to a girly girl, for a girlfriend, but Christie lit up his world in a way he had never known, and he needed to make sure she knew it.

"It's the earrings," she laughed. "Have I told you how much I love them?"

"Only about twice a day, since I gave them to you."

"I've been wearing them everywhere, even to the grocery."

"Then I must have done something right," he said.

"You do more than something right," she said. "You do all the things exceptionally well."

He got that grin in the corner of his mouth that she loved to see. It went with the assurance he had, being a SEAL.

Giving her hand a squeeze, he stopped, and turned to face her. "I'd like to talk about our future."

Our future?

She stood still, and caught her breath, holding it.

"I'd like you to be my woman, on a more permanent basis, if you're comfortable with that. Sort of a pre-engagement period. Let's try it for a year, and see where it takes us. No pressure, just more of what we've been doing."

"So, you won't see any other women, like in other ports, the way some of the guys do," she said.

"I would not. For me, there would be only you," he said.

"And I wouldn't see anyone else either," she said.

"Good," he nodded. "If you decided that you wanted to, you would tell me, and only then would we see other people. It's going to take good communication to make a long-distance relationship work, and with a SEAL that's what you will have. I'll be there when I can, but sometimes, I can't."

"I understand," she said. "Yes, this is what I want too. Let's try it."

"Excellent," he said. Then he bent down and kissed her, deep and long.

When they came up for air, her heart was racing.

They would have to walk back soon. Tanya had ridden with them, and they would need to take her home.

Reeds cell phone buzzed. He looked at the text. "Casper is giving Tanya a ride home, if that is okay with you," he said. "Though I don't know why he would need your permission."

"It's our code thing," she said. "Ask him for her word."

He typed in... Code word.

In a minute he got back... girdle.

He showed the screen to Christie, and she laughed.

"Why girdle?" Reed asked. "Or is it a secret."

"That's her code for, cut me out of my girdle now, I want to get naked with this man."

Reed laughed. Then he paused, looking at her, and asked, "Is that a code word you use, too?"

"Not me," she shook her head. "That is all Tanya. My code is lipstick, when I want to kiss a guy, and slow dance, when I want to make love. I'm more of a make love, than a get naked kind of woman."

"Slow dancing. I like it," he said. "So, Christie, now that we have the evening to ourselves, how about a little slow dancing?"

"Yes," she said, her smile spreading over her whole face. "I have been dreaming about slow dancing with you."

"Then by all means, let's make that dream come true." He winked at her.

Then hand in hand, they walked back to say goodnight to their hosts, moving faster this time, as both were rather impatient to get to that very special dance.

THE END

AFTERWORD

Thank you for taking the time to read *Real Movie Hero*.

If you enjoyed my story, please consider telling your friends and, or posting a review.

Word of mouth is an author's best friend, and reviews are so important to authors.

If you would be so kind as to leave a review and a rating on any website, this is the best way to thank and to encourage authors whose work you have enjoyed.

Please know, I appreciate and read every review.

Infinite love and gratitude,

Debra Parmley

SAMPLE CHAPTER: FINDING BRYCE,
CHAPTER ONE

Virginia Beach

"See you guys at Chicks?" Matthew Hunt "Matt" had opened the door, leaned in, and addressed Diesel and R.T. as they sat at two tables filling out paperwork.

"It's Kik's birthday," he reminded them.

Chicks Oyster Bar Marina was the favored place for SEAL Team Twelve to hang out when they were free to grab a beer and a bite to eat. Many celebrations through the years had been held there, from birthdays, to bachelor parties, and funeral wakes.

"Yeah," Tanner "Diesel" Taylor replied, then he held up the form he was filling out. "When these are done." He laid the paper down again and looked directly at Matt. "That was a clean op. Seems like there ought to be less paperwork instead of more, since we acquired the package and never had to fire one round."

Matt gave a nod, to acknowledge the comment and then said. "You're close to done. See you there."

A mostly by the book, no nonsense sort of man, dealing

with what is, was his way. Matt wasn't likely to engage in any kind of discussion about how things ought to be.

Diesel didn't usually complain about things, but he wasn't in his usual mood today. He filled out one more line and then pushed the form across the table to his buddy, Reed "Railroad" Tindall. "We ought to be out running maneuvers, not stuck here in the office doing paperwork."

Reed hated that nickname and was stuck with it, but Diesel had his own nickname for his buddy, and called him R.T. 'Short for railroad tracks' is what he said if anyone asked.

Tanner didn't mind his nickname one bit. Tanner "Diesel" Taylor earned his nickname the first week of basic, when he showed up with grease stains under his fingernails.

Working at his dad's repair shop every week during high school, he'd despaired of his hands, and how the pretty girls would turn him down for dates, thinking his hands were dirty. They didn't know a mechanic could scrub and scrub his hands, and still have stains.

Although it didn't take long for his Navy and SEAL training to wash away those stains, the nickname stuck, along with his ability to repair just about any kind of engine, even in the dark.

In his mind, it was just another skill, but as he'd only followed in his father's footsteps for one year after high school, he was as proud of carrying on his father's legacy into the armed force, as he was of carrying the name.

All the men in his father's side of the family had been mechanics, and his grandfather, and great grandfather had served in the Army during World Wars I and II, which was where they'd learned the ability to work on engines in the dark.

It wasn't that he hadn't wanted to follow in their footsteps even down to their military service, it was that he'd wanted to do more.

Serving as a SEAL was more. Much more.

And he loved every minute of it.

After SEAL training, Diesel never had trouble getting dates again. He was now a lady magnet. Just one of the things his latest girlfriend had more than a little trouble with.

Last night, Kari had broken up with him again, which meant he was free to see whoever he wanted to see.

Diesel watched as R.T. pulled that damn letter out of his pocket again, and with a sad expression, prepared to read the letter again.

"Hey man, you're not going to read that letter again, are you?" Diesel could've repeated most of the letter, having heard it often enough.

"I just don't understand why Becky called it off. She never explained, and she won't answer my phone calls." R.T. bent his head to the letter.

Damn. Dear John letters ought to be written in disappearing ink, or on exploding paper.

Diesel kept his thoughts to himself, but shook his head. Watching R.T, he got an idea.

"Hey. Saturday night. Got plans?"

"Nope." R.T, kept reading." Got laundry."

"You've got plans now." Diesel said. "You can do laundry some other time."

R.T. raised his head, and looked at Diesel.

Good. I got his attention away from that letter.

"Picture lots of chicks in skimpy Halloween costumes," Diesel said.

R.T. groaned. "Costumes?"

"Yeah. Costumes. Don't worry. This will be fun. Costume party is a masquerade."

"I don't have a costume, and there's not enough time to put one together."

"Got you covered. I know a place that rents them, and they're open tonight."

"I don't know, man. I ought to try calling Becky again."

"Come on. This party is a much better time than doing laundry, and crying into your beer. Gonna be plenty of ladies at this party. You know how chicks dig costumes."

"Yeah." R.T. had to admit they did. "Thanks Diesel."

Diesel nodded. "Welcome."

R.T. put the letter away, before picking up the pen again, to finish his task.

It didn't take them long to finish. Then they went home to change clothes, with a plan to meet up at the bar.

After they'd arrived at Chicks, before the other guys arrived, they went to sit out on the deck, and startled a seagull who'd perched on the railing hoping to find food.

The seagull was often there, in that spot. So often, that tourists coming to the marina had started feeding it. Now it came every night, expecting to find food.

The waitress who appeared soon after, to take their orders, had named the bird Fred. She claimed "Fred just wants to be fed."

"What'll you have, guys?" Sheri asked, with a wide smile, between two dimples.

The little waitress was an adorable bundle of energy, and currently dating an airline pilot, who was gone not quite as often as a SEAL would be.

"When are you going to trade that boyfriend in, for a real SEAL?" Diesel teased, already knowing what her answer would be.

"You guys are gone too often, and too long," she said, with a shake of her head, and a laugh.

All the guys teased her this way, and Diesel knew she liked it, though her answer was always the same.

Diesel thought her answer was a lot of hooey. Commercial pilots were gone a lot too, and a woman who could handle that, could handle dating a SEAL.

Women who couldn't, likely wouldn't be able to handle their man being on the road, for any job.

Some women needed more maintenance, just like some cars.

Kari was one of those women. But he and Kari were through.

Diesel enjoyed watching the boats dock at the Marina, which took his mind off Kari just like knocking back a few beers with the guys would take R.T.'s mind off that damn letter.

Cutter, and Matt joined them, and took seats.

"I'll buy a round," "Cutter" Antonius (Tony) Cuttino said.

"What are we celebrating?" R.T. asked.

"My winning at the casino last weekend," Cutter said.

"You have Italian connections?" Sheri asked with a giggle.

The guys knew Cutter had cousins with connections to a casino in New Jersey. When he went home to visit his grandmother, he'd visit the casino and come back with his wins.

"Did you bring me back any cannoli?" Sheri asked.

Last time he'd brought back cannoli his grandma had made.

"Not this time," he said. "Next time, cannoli for you, sweet." He gave her a wink.

She blushed and smiled.

The men placed their beer orders, and she hurried to the bar for their drinks.

"Any of you guys going to the costume party Saturday?" Diesel asked.

"Yeah," Matt said. "I'm gonna go as an IRS auditor."

"Really, man?" R.T. said. "What kind of costume is that?"

"An easy one. Just wear a suit and tie, and carry a calculator," Matt shrugged. "I even got business cards made up to hand out." He reached into his pocket, pulled one out, and handed it to R.T. "I'm here to audit your tax records," he said.

R.T. took the card, and glanced down at it. "That would scare the hell out of a lot of people," he said.

"You are so weird," Diesel shook his head.

"It's simple, cheap, and easy, and I'll have fun with it," Matt said with a shrug.

"That's what costume parties are for," Diesel nodded. "Having fun."

Just after Sheri delivered the beers, Rich, Osprey, and Enrique "Kik" Garcia joined them on the deck, and more beers were ordered.

"Add on some onion rings," Diesel said.

Sheri nodded, and headed for the kitchen.

"You going to the costume party, Rich?" Diesel asked.

"Nah. Costume parties aren't my thing," Richard "Rich" Irvine said.

One of the oldest members of the group, he'd turned down most invites to socialize, since getting back in touch with an old girlfriend from high school at his high school reunion. Now he spent most of his free time with her, trying to get out of the friend zone. She was hesitant about dating a SEAL.

All but Rich would attend the costume party.

Osprey was going as Robin Hood, and would carry a primitive bow he hunted with for fun, and Kik was going as Superman.

"Superman?" R.T. said. "I would've thought you'd want to go as Zorro, or something like that."

"Why, because I'm Latino?" Kik shook his head. He

smoothed his hair back with one hand, and then, reaching for a small section of his bangs, pulled it down, and made it curl. "I got the perfect hair. See? Superman."

All the guys laughed.

"Yeah, man," R.T. said. "I see it."

More SEAL brothers came in the door, which more than doubled the size of their gathering. The entire group was at Chicks tonight. All twenty SEALs.

Diesel glanced around the room. These twenty men were his brothers, and any one of them would have laid down his life for the other.

The Green Brotherhood was like no other, and he took a moment to take the sight of all his brothers in, creating a memory to savor in years to come.

The noise level in the bar rose, but the SEALs weren't the ones shouting and being rowdy.

They kept to themselves, and women in the bar were drawn to the strong silent warriors, like moths to flame. There was clearly something different about these men, the way they carried themselves, and the way they communicated amongst each other, often nonverbally, which set them apart. They exuded a quiet confidence, and their eyes were always taking in their surroundings with a quiet intelligence.

Craig McDonald "Big Mac" showed his Scots Irish heritage, by the multitude of freckles across his nose and cheeks, despite his deeply tanned face. It hid his ruddy complexion, and helped him blend in on their missions. Jet-black hair from his Irish mother saved him from having his fathers red hair, and allowed him to be picked for this special team.

To be on Team Twelve, you had to have dark hair as the team was often sent to South America, and needed to blend in. Blondes and redheads would stand out too much to be included. As a result, the men on Team Twelve could all be described as tall, dark, and handsome.

Blending in, in South America, was something Team Twelve did quite well.

Martin Lopez, the second Hispanic American on the team, was fluent in three languages, English, Spanish, and Portuguese. He was their go to man when it came to native dialects.

Chris Fenner "Fen" had almost gone to college on a chemistry scholarship, but he'd also wanted to become a SEAL. He was their best man with explosives, and a bit of a MacGyver, given his aptitude in chemistry.

He often said it was as much knowing what not to put together with another thing, as it was what to put together. He was also a pretty good cook, which he claimed also had to do with chemistry.

Daniel "Tractor" Edwards grew up on a hay farm, and would have been a fourth-generation farmer, if he'd stayed home on the farm instead of joining the SEALs.

His father had a John Deere collection that men traveled miles to see. Daniel had made the mistake of talking about it too often, early in his training, was handed the nickname "Tractor" and it stuck.

His best buddy in training told him it could've been worse; they could've saddled him with "Farm-boy."

Adam "DaVinci" Burgess was always drawing and doodling, with a pen, or pencil. Tonight, he was already drawing on his cocktail napkin before he'd finished his first beer.

It would have been easy to sit and watch him, instead of focusing on the hot young woman standing nearby, hoping for attention.

Thomas (Tom) Campbell "Soupman" got his nickname after explaining the way to spell his last name, was "Like the soup, man." Once the nickname stuck it was stuck good.

Scott Roberts, "Casper" was like a ghost. He could enter a room and then leave it, without anyone knowing he'd been there.

James Slater "Slim Jim" was a skinny man with toned muscles. His metabolism was so high, he could eat anything and not gain one pound of weight.

Sawyer "Pipes" Ferguson played the bagpipes with the local Scottish group, and sometimes wore a kilt, if performing with the group for weddings or funeral services.

Sam Valente, an Italian American known as "Sammie the Conductor" because of the expressive way he used his hands when he talked, was gesturing animatedly tonight, something he did when he'd drank enough beer.

Peter "Buzz" Horne had a weird snore that sounded like a low buzz.

Jocko "Numbers" Lewis was so good with numbers, they didn't need a calculator when he was around.

And Jake Summers "Oscar" could act any part, and make it believable.

But really, all these men were actors capable of blending in, making anyone believe they were who they pretended to be, and doing what it took to complete a mission.

They were a special team of Navy SEALs, one that few outside the SEAL Teams had ever heard of.

Tonight, they were all at the bar, because it was the rotation of their cycle to have them back in Virginia, before they cycled out again into the next phase. And it just happened to be Kik's birthday.

The beer was flowing, the noise level was rising, and if the good time Kik seemed to be having was any indication, he was going to have a huge hangover tomorrow.

Ordinarily, had he been back home with his family,

there would have been a large family party, with a barbe-cued goat, music, and beer. After he joined the SEAL team, he'd continued to invite every one of his brothers to cele-brate his birthday, and if they were available, they would join in.

Kik was having the time of his life tonight.

All the men trained hard, worked hard, and partied hard.

By the end of the evening, they made sure Kik made it home safe, as he was in no shape to drive, and the bar emptied out, the only occupant left on the patio, a lone seagull with the nickname of Fred, who had returned, hoping for leftovers to eat.

"Come on Pippa, this is the best party of the year, and everyone will be in costume," Cheryl said. "No one will know who you are. It's the perfect chance."

It was only the tenth time Cheryl had asked her to go to the Halloween party.

Finally, tired of being bugged about it, Pippa said, "Okay, I'll go."

"Great!" Cheryl's eyes widened, and she grabbed both of Pippa's hands, squeezing tight as she bounced on her heels. "You're going to be so glad you changed your mind. We're going to have a blast."

For once, Pippa would take a page from her mother's diary, and live in the moment.

As her mother had said, "Joyce, my dear, you haven't yet learned that life must be grasped in the moment."

Joyce Pippalousa Smith never gave out her birth name. Her full middle name had always been an embarrassment to her, though she did like her daddy's nickname for her.

He was the only one to call her "Pippa", and she missed him dearly. Her mother had always called her Joyce.

After her mother had made her announcement, she'd gone sailing off to Hawaii with a new man, who kept a boat at his summer home. "Waiting just gives you more likelihood you'll miss out. Your father may be dead, but I'm not."

Her mother was the kind of woman who couldn't stand to be alone, and one of her friends had been waiting in the wings, ready to date her.

Thinking back to the huge blow-up Pippa and her younger sister, Jeanie Magic Smith, had with their mother the day before their mother left town, made Pippa wonder where her mother was now, and reminded her, she needed to call Jeanie this weekend, and get caught up.

Mother could be anywhere. I have no idea how to reach her at sea. I don't even have her new number.

But as Jeanie often said, 'The phone works both ways.' And her sister's number hadn't changed.

Though usually Pippa was the one who had to call her sister. Months could go by, if she didn't, before Jeanie got around to calling her.

For once, Pippa was going to take a page from her mother's book. She was going to live a little.

It had been a long time since she'd gone out and had fun, and she'd always loved costume parties and Halloween.

"Now, what are you gonna be?" Cheryl asked.

"I don't know. I haven't had time to think about it," Pippa said, her tone wry. She'd only agreed a second ago.

Cheryl waved a hand, and continued in her rapid-fire way; clearly thrilled Pippa was going. "We can go to the costume shop after we get off work."

"Okay," Pippa said.

A masquerade party seemed safe enough. It was unlikely that her ex would be there. She'd moved several states away from Stan Nitty, and hoped to never see him again.

After work, they headed to That Magical Place, a store which sold costumes, and decorations for Halloween.

"Do you have any sexy costumes for women?" Cheryl asked.

The clerk grinned. "Yes, we do. Follow me, and I'll show you. Do you have any themes in mind?"

"I looked up your selections online. I think I'd like to be a woodland fairy," Pippa said. "With wings, and pointed ears, and everything." Now that she was getting excited about going, why not go full-on fantasy?

"Oh, fun," Cheryl said. "I'm going as a sexy nurse. Maybe I can play nurse with one of those hot Navy SEALs tomorrow night. Is your costume going to be sexy?"

"Well..." Pippa considered the costume she remembered from the website. "It's short and shows a lot of leg, and a lot of cleavage. It's also cheap, which I need. I don't have much budget for a costume."

"Want me to help you with your makeup and hair?"

"Oh, would you? That would be awesome." Pippa knew Cheryl was good at doing hair and makeup.

"Yeah, I'll come over an hour before and help you get ready," Cheryl said.

"Thanks, Cheryl." As she did every day, Pippa thanked her instincts for bringing her here to Virginia. Her sister had been only too willing to give her safe harbor when she'd needed it, and she lived just an hour away.

"No problem, Miss Pipp."

Pippa wrinkled her nose. "You're not gonna call me that at the party, I hope."

"No, I'm not gonna call you at all, 'til we agree it's time to go home. We're gonna circulate as single ladies, so the men will be more likely to approach us," Cheryl winked.

"Oh, right," Pippa nodded. "Good thinking."

The next day, Pippa's cousin Louise called her at work and left a message for her to call back. Far from being a normal call, Louise would only have called if someone had died or something very big had happened. So as Pippa called Louise back, she held her breath. "Hey, Louise. What's happened?"

"This time it's good news, Pippa," Louise said. "You won't have to worry about Stan anymore. He's been sent to prison for three years. Felonious assault. He beat up a guy in a bar. That was bad enough. But then he went back and beat him some more. The guy was hurt bad, and they had to call an ambulance. Stan claimed it wasn't his fault, and the other guy did this and did that, but everything was caught on the bar's security cameras. And it didn't hurt that they had pictures of the bruises he left on your neck, or that you have a restraining order out on him, already on record. He's obviously a violent and dangerous man. I'm so glad he's been sent to prison and won't be out for a long time. I couldn't wait to tell you."

Pippa breathed a sigh of relief. Stress began to drain out of her body. "Oh, that is good news. He can't find me now, and suddenly show up on my doorstep to hurt me. Not while he's in prison. So, I'm safe. Finally. No more looking over my shoulder, worrying he might be the man in the baseball cap behind me. I'm safe, finally safe!"

She felt like dancing and spinning around the room.

"Yes, you are," Louise said. "Does this mean you'll come home, now?"

"I am home," Pippa said. "Virginia is my home now, and I just started taking a couple college classes."

"So, you're staying?"

"Yes." Pippa didn't say that she never wanted to move back to her hometown, but she surely felt that way. She'd escaped a horrible marriage, a depressing house, and a town, which lost more jobs every year, and she never wanted to go back.

There was no future there. Only the past. And the past was over and done. Finally.

"Well, all right. If that's what you want," Louise said. "I just want you to be happy."

"Oh, I am happy," Pippa said. "Happier than I've been in a very long time."

The night of the party, Pippa let Cheryl into her apartment, and they went straight into her bathroom, where she had a curling iron already plugged in. She wanted to look different tonight, and her long brown hair usually hung straight. Most days, she loved a wash-and-go kind of lifestyle and rarely wore makeup. But tonight, she wanted a little glamour—her hair curling, smoky-sparkling makeup, and fairy ears glued onto her ears.

Cheryl curled Pippa's hair until it had ringlets at the ends, which gave it a whole lot more body. Once she finished applying makeup to Pippa's face, Cheryl took gold glitter and sprinkled it in Pippa's hair and across her bared shoulders. Spaghetti straps held the silky fairy dress up, leaving a lot of skin bare. The way the dress was cut in back, there was no way to wear a bra with this one.

It was the most daring thing Pippa had ever worn in public.

"Might as well use it up," said Cheryl before sprinkling the rest of the vial of glitter down Pippa's cleavage.

Pippa felt the glitter whisper between her breasts. "Cheryl!" she said, laughing. "I don't need it everywhere."

"Oh, but I think you do," Cheryl said. "Keep him looking for the end of that glitter trail, and you'll have his attention for sure. Then he'll be hard at attention, and you'll have some real fun."

Pippa kept chuckling. "I'll bedazzle him with my cleavage."

"You know it." Cheryl winked and tossed the empty container into the trashcan. "Ready to go?"

"Yes, I just need my tiny purse."

"Here." Cheryl reached into her purse for two condoms and handed them to Pippa. "Be prepared, because those Navy boys are not always like boy scouts, and some of them really get around."

"Oh, right." They hadn't talked much about Pippa's former life, only that she'd divorced a man who was no good and that she was trying to make a new life without complications. She hadn't hinted at her ex's violent tendencies.

Cheryl, being a party girl, understood the "no complications" bit. She never dated a guy longer than six months. Said it got claustrophobic if they lingered any longer.

"Thanks. I hadn't thought to pick those up," Pippa said.

"Always keep one in your purse and some in your nightstand. Tonight's a chance for you to have fun without the hassle of a date. But if you need more than two of these, you're on your own, girlfriend."

Unable to stop a blush, Pippa shook her head. "I won't need more than two."

I'll be lucky to need one, she thought. It had been over a year since she'd had sex, and she missed it. In the good times, at the beginning of her marriage, before everything went terribly bad, sex had been good, with that rush of attraction that went straight to her core, lighting everything up, just like fairy lights. It had been magic.

I want that again, even if for just one night. This is a start. And no one will even know who I am. This is perfect.

ACKNOWLEDGMENTS

Thank you to all who helped make this book possible.

To USMC veteran Jacob Romo for the class on situational awareness, and self defense classes. To USMC veteran Charles "Tazz" Welshans for advice on Marines and gunfights. To Army veteran, Robert Arrow, aka Bobby, my gun instructor, friend and sometimes co-writer. I could not have written these gun scenes as well, without you.

To Navy SEAL veteran Bill Hellman, for advice on SEALs and guidance with developing my new Green Brotherhood: SEAL Team XII series.

To all previous editors and early readers of my novella, *Split Screen Scream,* which was the seed for this revised story, *Real Movie Hero*, and the new series. You wanted to read more of the story and now, here it is, with a SEAL Team of twenty men and many more stories to follow.

To Sheri L. McGathy, my cover artist, for all the covers for the new series and the series logo.

To my assistant, Melissa Ammons, who helps me with numerous things, so I can write.

Thank you to my family, and especially my husband, for love and support through all these years together, for the

adventures and journeys we have taken and are still taking,
and for making it possible for me to write so many books.
May the adventures continue.

Special thanks to my readers.

I love you all.

ABOUT THE AUTHOR

Debra Parmley is an adventurous, multi-genre author who lives in a motorhome full-time, with her husband, as they travel the U.S.A.

An Air Force veteran's wife, Debra writes military romantic suspense. She also writes contemporary romance, holiday romance, fairytale romance, 1920's romance, gritty western historical romance, futuristic romance, and time travel romance.

Debra says "Every day we are alive is a beautiful day," and she likes to give her readers and her story people a story that ends happily.

Her first romance, A Desperate Journey, a gritty western historical, was published in 2008 in eBook, and 2009 in print, after being selected as one of the novels to compete in the American Title II contest put on by Dorchester Publishing, and Romantic Times Book Lovers magazine. One year later, her agent sold the book in a traditional deal to a small press.

Debra has sold travel, walked the plank of a pirate ship, off the coast of Grand Cayman, swum with dolphins in Moorea in French Polynesia, escorted a bus full of people through Scotland, and set foot in over 13 countries.

She married her high school sweetheart, whom she asked out on a five-dollar bet. After living in several states with her husband and two sons, and then living for 23 years just outside Memphis, TN, in Bartlett, she and her husband sold their home and moved into a 43-foot motorhome, a Tin Allegro bus, where they live full-time.

In the summer of 2022, they lived and worked on a sandbar, in Rodanthe, on Hatteras Island, in the outer banks of North Carolina. In early 2023, they worked as gate guards, guarding oil rigs in Texas. Their current adventure is living and working for six months in Cody, Wyoming, the rodeo capitol of the world. Then they will be off on their next adventure.

Debra writes about their travels and is working on a book about their first year on the read.

For more about her travels, visit her Beautiful Day Traveler blog or her YouTube Channel.

As Debra Bishop, she writes fairy tales for all ages, fantasy, and children's books.

www.debraparmley.com

ALSO BY DEBRA PARMLEY

ROMANTIC SUSPENSE:

Military Romantic Suspense:

Green Brotherhood SEAL Team XII:

Finding Bryce, book one - eBook, paperback

Real Movie Hero, book two – eBook, paperback

Saving the Bellydancer, book three – eBook, paperback

Brotherhood Protectors series:

Montana Marine - eBook, paperback

Defensive Instructor - eBook, paperback

Marine Protector - eBook, paperback

Blind Trust - eBook, paperback

A Triple C Ranch Christmas Wedding - eBook, paperback

Montana Delta Rescue - eBook, paperback

Montana SEAL Protector - eBook, paperback

White Horse Wedding – eBook, paperback - 2023

Montana Rodeo Protector - eBook, paperback – 2023

Romantic Suspense:

Bobbins Sisters Trilogy:

Check Out – book one, eBook, paperback, audiobook

Check In – book two, eBook, paperback

Check Up – book three, 2023

Single Title:

Aboard the Wishing Star - eBook, paperback, audiobook

Jenna's Christmas Wish - eBook, paperback

To Catch an Elf – 2023

HISTORICAL ROMANCE:

Western Historical Romance:

Gone to Texas: A Desperate Journey - (original, sweeter version) - Large Print Hardcover, eBook, paperback

Dangerous Ties - eBook, paperback, audiobook

Deadly Adversaries - eBook, paperback

Desperate, Dangerous, Deadly: A Western Collection – eBook

Isabella, Bride of Ohio: American Mail Order Bride – (sweeter version) - Large Print Hardcover, eBook, paperback

Penny From Deadwood – eBook, paperback 2023

1920's Romance:

Trapping the Butterfly – book one, eBook, paperback, audiobook, Large Print Hardcover

Dancing Butterfly – book two, eBook, paperback

Exotic Butterfly – book three, 2024

FAIRY TALE AND FANTASY ROMANCE:

The Twelve Stitches of Christmas – (short story) – eBook

Vague Directions - eBook, paperback- 2023

FUTURISTIC DYSTOPIAN ROMANCE

The Hunger Roads Trilogy:

Another Change of Scenery – 2023

Down a Back Road – 2023

Into the Convergence Zone – 2024

POETRY

Poetry Anthology:

Twilight Dips – eBook, print

NONFICTION:

Travel Memoir:

Anywhere But Here: Our First Year Living on the Road - 2023

OUT OF PRINT:

Protecting Pippa

Split Screen Scream

Protecting Zarifah

Vague Directions – short story

A Desperate Journey

Isabella, Bride of Ohio

Tales From Deadwood - anthology

We Know the Truth, Do You? Area 51 – anthology (going to the moon/time capsule)

Wounded Heroes - anthology

Hansel & Gretel: Down the Rabbit Hole – anthology

More Monsters from Memphis – anthology

WRITING AS DEBRA BISHOP:

Fairytales for all ages:

The Sweetest Day - fairytale Hansel and Gretel story, eBook, paperback

Fantasy:

The Rolling House – time travel serial fiction on Kindle Vella

Gatalop – 2024

Bellserie – 2024

Children's stories, coming 2024

www.ingramcontent.com/pod-product-compliance
Lightning Source LLC
Chambersburg PA
CBHW030754200726
48288CB00004B/1169